The Silent Hand's Illusion

This is a work of fiction. Similarities to real people, places, or events are entirely coincidental.

THE SILENT HAND: BEHIND THE MARKET'S ILLUSION

First edition. October 21, 2024.

Copyright © 2024 Smita Singh.

ISBN: 979-8227066749

Written by Smita Singh.

Dear Reader,

When we think about the stock market, images of bustling trading floors, fast-ticking numbers, and endless charts come to mind. To many, it's a place of opportunity—a platform where fortunes are made, dreams are realized, and hard work pays off in the form of rising stock prices. But beneath the surface lies a different reality, one shrouded in manipulation, deception, and power plays that most of us will never see.

"The Silent Hand: Behind the Market's Illusion" is not just a story about stock market manipulation; it's a window into a world where the movements of a few can change the fate of many. It's a world where vast sums of money, hidden political ties, and the control of information dictate who wins and who loses—often leaving small traders holding the short end of the stick.

I was inspired to write this book after hearing stories from traders who had lost everything in market crashes that seemed to defy logic. As I dug deeper, I began to understand the extent of influence that big capital and political power have on markets. It's a game designed to be unwinnable for the little guy, yet millions of people play it every day, unaware of the forces working against them.

This book follows the journey of Arjun, a journalist who stumbles upon this hidden world and embarks on a quest to expose the truth. Through his eyes, we'll see how a nexus of powerful individuals—the politicians, financiers, and media moguls—manipulate the market to serve their own interests, creating illusions that trap unsuspecting traders.

As you read Arjun's story, you might find yourself questioning whether such manipulation exists in the real world. The truth is, financial markets are far more complex than they appear. While the characters and events in this book are fictional, the mechanisms of manipulation they expose are very real.

I hope this story sheds light on the often invisible forces that shape our markets and inspires you to think critically about the narratives we're fed. The stock market, like many systems, is built on trust, but that trust can be easily broken when power and greed take the reins.

Thank you for joining me on this journey into the shadows of the financial world. I hope you find this book both enlightening and thrilling.

Stay curious, stay informed, and remember: the market is never as free as it seems.

Warm regards,
Smita Singh

Chapter 1: "Whispers in the Alley"

Chapter 2: "The House Always Wins"

Chapter 3: "Echoes in the Numbers"

Chapter 4: "Smoke and Mirrors"

Chapter 5: "The Media Mirage"

Chapter 6: "The Shark Tank"

Chapter 7: "The Secret Ledger"

Chapter 8: "A Wolf in the Shadows"

Chapter 9: "The Masked Markets"

Chapter 10: "The Glass Ceiling Shatters"

Chapter 11: "Rats Abandon the Ship"

Chapter 12: "The Calm After the Crash"

Chapter 1: Whispers in the Alley

The narrow alley was uninviting, its dimly lit path lined with the debris of a bustling city that seemed too busy to notice the shadows it harbored. The air was thick with the scent of damp concrete, and the hum of distant traffic created an eerie backdrop to Arjun's hurried steps. His heart raced slightly—not out of fear, but anticipation. He had been in darker places before, chasing stories that threatened to uncover corruption, but this felt different. This time, the stakes were higher. His gut told him that tonight might change everything.

The message had come late in the evening, a cryptic note dropped into his email inbox, sent from an anonymous source. The content was brief but enough to spark his curiosity: *"Meet me at the Black Rose Alley. You want the truth about the market. I know what you're looking for."*

The Black Rose Alley wasn't the kind of place Arjun frequented, but as a seasoned investigative journalist, he had learned that the most important stories often came from the most unlikely sources. The email had mentioned something about market manipulation, something Arjun was already suspicious of. He had seen the data, the sudden and violent price movements that didn't align with any rational market behavior. But it wasn't until now that he had a lead—an actual human source who could potentially confirm his suspicions.

As he turned the corner, entering the alley, Arjun's eyes scanned the darkened surroundings. A solitary streetlamp flickered, casting a yellow glow over the entrance to the alley, while the rest was swallowed by shadows. He could hear the faint sound of footsteps approaching, but no one was in sight yet. His grip tightened on the small notebook he always carried, ready to document any details that might lead him closer to the truth.

THE SILENT HAND: BEHIND THE MARKET'S ILLUSION 5

From the far end of the alley, a figure emerged from the shadows. The man was of average build, wearing a plain hoodie that obscured his face in the dim light. His pace was slow and deliberate, as if he were assessing the situation just as much as Arjun was. When the man came closer, Arjun could finally see his face—pale, with dark circles under his eyes, and an expression of unease.

"You're the journalist, right? Arjun Verma?" the man asked in a low, cautious tone.

Arjun nodded. "And you're the one who sent the email."

The man glanced over his shoulder, as though making sure they weren't being watched, before gesturing to a spot farther down the alley, away from the prying eyes of the street. "I don't have much time. We have to be quick."

Arjun followed him to a quieter corner, where the shadows swallowed them whole. His senses were heightened, every sound amplified, every movement magnified. He could feel the tension rolling off the man in waves. Whoever he was, he was scared. That much was clear.

"You said you had information about the market. Something that could explain the recent volatility?" Arjun began, keeping his voice steady. He didn't want to spook the man, but he needed answers.

The man exhaled slowly, his breath visible in the cool night air. "Yeah, more than just volatility," he muttered, his voice barely above a whisper. "You're right. Something's off. The market—it's not free. It hasn't been for a long time."

Arjun's pulse quickened. "What do you mean? Are you talking about manipulation? Insider trading?"

The man shook his head, his gaze darting around the alley as if expecting someone to appear at any moment. "It's bigger than that. It's systematic. There's a group—a syndicate—that controls the entire thing. They've got their hands in everything: finance, politics, media. They create the illusions, the fake moves. They make the market look like it's responding to real events, but it's all orchestrated. Every rise, every fall—it's all planned."

Arjun's mind raced as he processed the man's words. A syndicate? The idea of market manipulation wasn't new, but on this scale? Involving not just traders and hedge funds but politicians and media moguls? It was almost too much to believe.

"Who are these people? This syndicate you're talking about?" Arjun pressed.

The man hesitated, his eyes narrowing as if weighing the consequences of what he was about to reveal. "They're untouchable. They're the ones with the real power. The ones who can make or break markets with a single move. They control the flow of money—black money. They use it to influence everything, from corporate mergers to government policies. And they're laundering it through the stock market. That's how they clean it."

Arjun felt a chill crawl down his spine. He had suspected manipulation, but this was far worse. The idea that the stock market, the bedrock of modern capitalism, was being used as a laundromat for dirty money was staggering.

"Who's behind it?" Arjun asked, his voice sharper now. "Names. I need names."

The man glanced around again, his paranoia growing by the second. "I can't give you all the names. But there's one you should know—everyone in the business knows it, even if they don't say it out loud. They call themselves *The Syndicate*. It's made up of some of the most powerful people in the world. Hedge fund managers, politicians, corporate executives, and media moguls. They all work together. They move money, they control the narrative, and they profit from both sides. They're untouchable because they've got everyone in their pocket. If you dig too deep, they'll bury you."

Arjun scribbled furiously in his notebook, his heart pounding as he realized the gravity of what he was hearing. This wasn't just a financial story—it was a political one, a criminal one. If what this man was saying was true, it meant that the entire system was rigged, from the highest levels of government down to the individual stock trades. And the small traders—the everyday people putting their money into the market, believing in the promise of free enterprise—they were nothing more than pawns in a much larger game.

"How do they do it?" Arjun asked. "How do they manipulate the market without getting caught?"

The man ran a hand through his hair, his face lined with stress. "It's all in the algorithms. They use high-frequency trading to move the market in ways that are almost impossible to detect. They place massive orders and then cancel them at the last second, creating artificial demand or supply. The prices move, the small traders follow, and just when everyone thinks they've figured it out, the syndicate pulls the rug out from under them. They've got the money and the technology to do it on a scale no one can match."

Arjun felt a knot tightening in his stomach. He had read about high-frequency trading before—how powerful algorithms could execute trades in fractions of a second, far faster than any human could react. But he had never imagined that such technology could be used to orchestrate a grand manipulation of the entire market.

"And the politicians?" Arjun asked. "How are they involved?"

The man smirked bitterly. "You really think politicians aren't in on it? Some of them are part of the syndicate, sitting in the finance ministry, passing laws that protect these guys. They make sure no one can touch them. And in return, they get a cut of the profits, plus campaign donations and all the influence they could ever want."

The revelation hit Arjun like a punch to the gut. He had always been skeptical of politicians and their cozy relationships with big business, but this went far beyond mere corruption. If politicians were actively working with the syndicate to protect their operations, then the entire system was compromised. It wasn't just about money—it was about power, control, and the ability to shape entire economies at will.

As Arjun absorbed the weight of the man's words, he realized that he was standing at the edge of a story that could shake the foundations of the financial world. But with that realization came a surge of fear. If this syndicate was as powerful as the man claimed, then exposing them wouldn't be easy. They had the money, the technology, and the political connections to silence anyone who got too close.

"Why are you telling me this?" Arjun asked, his voice steady but his mind racing.

The man's eyes flickered with a mix of fear and desperation. "Because I'm done. I've been part of this system for too long, and I've seen too much. I can't live with it anymore. They've ruined too many lives, destroyed too many people. I thought I could ignore it, but it's eating me up inside. I need to get out. And I need someone to tell the world what's really happening."

Arjun nodded, his mind already working on how to piece together the story. "But why me? Why not go to the authorities?"

The man chuckled darkly. "The authorities? They're in on it too. The regulators, the watchdogs—they've all been bought. They'll look the other way, or worse, they'll come after me for speaking out. No, you're my only shot. You're the only one who can expose this. But you have to be careful. These people don't play by the rules. If they find out you're investigating them, they'll come for you. And they won't stop until you're gone."

The weight of the man's words hung heavy in the air as Arjun considered the risks. He had chased dangerous stories before, but this was different. The syndicate wasn't just a group of corrupt businessmen—they were a global force, a shadowy network that could crush anyone who threatened their empire.

"Alright," Arjun said finally, his voice firm. "I'll look into it. But I need more. I need evidence. Something solid that I can use to back up your claims."

The man nodded, his face etched with relief. "I'll get it to you. But be careful, Arjun. You're walking into a minefield, and the people who laid the traps—they don't miss."

As the man turned to leave, disappearing back into the shadows of the alley, Arjun felt a surge of adrenaline. The story he had been chasing for months was finally within reach, but with it came a terrifying realization: he was about to go up against forces far more powerful than he had ever imagined.

The calm before the storm had passed. Now, the storm was about to begin.

Chapter 2: "The House Always Wins"

The world of high finance was built on the illusion of fairness, where every player had an equal opportunity to profit from the market. For the average investor, the stock market was supposed to be a place of opportunity—a game of strategy, intuition, and timing. But as Arjun dug deeper into the web of manipulation revealed by the whistleblower, it became painfully clear that this so-called game was rigged. It wasn't a fair fight. The house always won, and the house was controlled by The Syndicate.

Arjun sat in his dimly lit office, the glow of his computer screen illuminating the room as he pored over endless charts, trade logs, and news articles. His editor had given him space to work on this story, understanding the potential it held. If what he was uncovering was true, this could blow the lid off the entire financial system. But it wasn't just about the story anymore—Arjun was now personally invested. He couldn't shake the feeling that he was on the verge of something massive.

The whistleblower's words kept ringing in his ears: *"They make the market look like it's responding to real events, but it's all orchestrated."*

He had been investigating stock market volatility for weeks now, and it had become increasingly clear that some of the recent market movements made no sense. Stocks were rising and falling with dizzying speed, but these shifts weren't being driven by any news or earnings reports. The broader economic picture didn't justify such wild swings either. It was as if an invisible hand was pulling the strings.

Arjun leaned back in his chair, thinking about the mechanics of market manipulation. How did The Syndicate do it? How did they move the market in a way that trapped smaller traders, leaving them with devastating losses while the big players walked away with massive profits? He knew that answering these questions would be key to blowing this story wide open.

The stock market is often compared to a casino, but for Arjun, it was becoming clear that the analogy didn't fully capture the level of manipulation at play. In a casino, at least, the odds were known. The roulette wheel spins, and there are clear probabilities for each outcome. But in the stock market, the odds were being secretly shifted by The Syndicate, tilting the game in their favor without anyone realizing it.

Arjun started tracing specific trades, using publicly available data from stock exchanges. He knew that many high-frequency trades happened in microseconds, so he needed to focus on larger, more visible patterns. The ones that left a trace. As he sifted through the data, something caught his eye—a series of trades that seemed to follow an unusual pattern.

A particular stock—one that had been relatively stable for months—suddenly plummeted in value during a single trading session. Small traders, sensing danger, panicked and sold off their shares en masse. But just minutes later, the stock rebounded sharply, regaining most of its value by the end of the day. The result? Countless small traders were wiped out, their portfolios bleeding from the steep sell-off, while those who held their positions—or even worse, shorted the stock during its plunge—made huge profits.

It wasn't just a fluke. Arjun found similar patterns in several other stocks. The moves were fast, precise, and carefully timed to trigger panic selling. And every time, it was the small traders who bore the brunt of the losses, while The Syndicate—and their army of algorithmic traders—swooped in to profit from the carnage.

To understand how The Syndicate executed these traps, Arjun needed to delve deeper into the mechanics of market manipulation. He reached out to an old contact from his days as a financial journalist—a retired trader who had worked for one of the biggest

hedge funds in the country. The trader, Rajesh, was known for his expertise in technical analysis and had seen the rise of high-frequency trading firsthand.

They met at a small café in the financial district, far from the sleek skyscrapers that housed the offices of the world's most powerful traders. Rajesh had aged since Arjun had last seen him, but his eyes were still sharp, scanning the room with the instinct of someone who had spent years navigating the treacherous waters of Wall Street.

"Long time, Arjun. What's this about?" Rajesh asked as he sipped his coffee.

Arjun wasted no time, pulling out his notebook and showing Rajesh the charts he had been studying. "I'm working on a story. I've been seeing these strange patterns in the market—stocks crashing and then bouncing back within minutes. It's wiping out small traders, but the big players seem to be making a killing. I think it's deliberate. I think it's a trap."

Rajesh studied the charts for a moment, then nodded. "You're not wrong. What you're seeing is classic market manipulation, but on a scale most people can't even imagine. It's not new either—this kind of thing has been happening for years, but it's become more sophisticated with the rise of high-frequency trading."

"How does it work?" Arjun asked.

Rajesh leaned forward, lowering his voice as if to shield their conversation from prying ears. "The key is liquidity. The big players, like hedge funds and institutional investors, have access to massive amounts of capital. They can use that capital to flood the market with buy or sell orders, creating an artificial demand or supply. When they want to drive a stock price down, they start selling—big blocks of shares, all at once. The small traders see the price dropping and panic, thinking something's wrong. They sell too, driving the price even lower."

"And then?" Arjun asked, his pen poised over his notebook.

"Then, once the price has dropped to a certain level—just when the small traders have sold everything and taken their losses—the big players swoop in and start buying again. They've created the perfect buying opportunity for themselves. The stock rebounds, and they make a fortune. The small traders, meanwhile, are left with nothing but losses."

Arjun nodded, his mind racing. "But it's not just about the trades, is it? There's something bigger going on."

Rajesh smiled grimly. "You're catching on. It's not just about moving the stock price. The Syndicate has the power to control the narrative, too. They've got their hands in the media, in politics. They can plant stories, create false rumors, even manipulate economic reports. They'll make it look like there's a legitimate reason for the stock's drop—a bad earnings report, a negative news article, whatever they need to get the small traders to panic."

Arjun felt a chill run down his spine. It was worse than he thought. This wasn't just about financial manipulation—it was a coordinated effort to control the entire market, from the prices of individual stocks to the information that traders used to make their decisions.

The conversation with Rajesh opened Arjun's eyes to the complexity of the system he was up against, but he still needed to understand the role of technology in all of this. He had heard about high-frequency trading (HFT) before, but it was always discussed in abstract terms. He needed to see it in action to fully grasp how The Syndicate was using it to manipulate the market.

High-frequency trading was the cutting edge of modern finance. It involved the use of powerful algorithms and supercomputers to execute trades at lightning-fast speeds—thousands of trades in the blink of an eye. These algorithms could detect tiny movements in stock prices and exploit them for profit, often before human traders even realized what was happening. And The Syndicate, with its vast resources, was the master of this game.

Arjun managed to get access to a small HFT firm through a contact who worked in technology journalism. The firm was located in a nondescript office building in the heart of the city, its exterior giving no indication of the billions of dollars that flowed through its systems every day. Inside, rows of computer screens filled the room, displaying complex charts, code, and real-time stock data. It was a world Arjun barely understood, but he could feel the power emanating from the machines.

The head of the firm, a tech-savvy entrepreneur named Vikram, agreed to give Arjun a tour, though he was careful to keep the details of their trading strategies under wraps.

"We're essentially looking for microsecond inefficiencies in the market," Vikram explained as they walked through the trading floor. "Our algorithms are programmed to detect tiny price discrepancies—fractions of a cent—and exploit them. We place millions of trades every day, all in the span of milliseconds."

"And these algorithms," Arjun asked, "they're completely automated? No human intervention?"

"Exactly," Vikram replied. "Humans are too slow. By the time a human trader reacts, the opportunity is gone. That's why high-frequency trading has taken over—it's all about speed."

Arjun watched as the traders monitored their screens, their fingers hovering over keyboards but rarely typing. The algorithms were doing all the work. But it wasn't just speed that mattered—it was control. These algorithms weren't just reacting to the market; they were shaping it. With enough capital, an HFT firm could place massive buy or sell orders in a matter of seconds, causing prices to move and triggering reactions from other traders. It was the ultimate form of manipulation, and The Syndicate had mastered it.

Back in his office, Arjun began tracing the unnatural trades he had identified earlier, using the insights he had gained from Rajesh and the HFT firm. The pattern was becoming clearer. The Syndicate's algorithmic traders would enter the market with massive trades, creating a ripple effect that spread across the entire stock exchange. Small traders, relying on outdated tools and delayed information, would see the movement and react, thinking they were catching a real trend.

But by the time they acted, it was already too late. The trend was an illusion, created by The Syndicate to lure them in. The stock would either reverse course or stabilize, leaving the small traders on the wrong side of the trade. Their losses were The Syndicate's gains.

Arjun's investigation was uncovering a hidden world of market manipulation that few people outside the financial elite even knew existed. The game was rigged, and the small traders never stood a chance.

But Arjun knew that exposing this story wouldn't be easy. The Syndicate's reach was vast, and they had the power to crush anyone who threatened their empire. He was about to enter the most dangerous phase of his investigation, and there was no turning back.

The house always wins. But for the first time, Arjun was determined to change the rules of the game

Chapter 3: "Echoes in the Numbers"

Arjun sat at his desk, the weight of the investigation pressing down on him. He had spent weeks gathering data, following leads, and talking to experts like Rajesh, but the deeper he went, the more elusive the truth seemed. He had uncovered patterns of market manipulation, clear evidence that The Syndicate was using its vast capital to control the market, but he needed hard proof. He needed the numbers.

That's where Maya came in.

Maya was a data analyst Arjun had met years ago during a financial investigation. Brilliant and meticulous, she had an uncanny ability to find meaning in the chaos of data. Arjun had called her in to help him analyze the mountain of trading information he had collected. If anyone could make sense of the irregular patterns he was seeing, it was her.

Maya's office was tucked away in a modest building on the outskirts of the financial district, far from the glass towers of the major trading firms. Arjun arrived late in the afternoon, greeted by the soft hum of computers and the clatter of keyboards as Maya's team of analysts worked on various projects. She had built a reputation as one of the best data scientists in the business, taking on cases that others deemed too complex to crack.

Arjun found her sitting in front of a massive screen, the flicker of code reflected in her glasses. She didn't look up when he walked in, her fingers flying across the keyboard as she ran one last query.

"Give me a minute," she said without turning around.

Arjun waited, watching as lines of data streamed across the screen. After a moment, she leaned back in her chair and stretched.

Finally, she turned to him and smiled. "Arjun, it's been a while. What do you have for me this time?"

He handed her a folder containing printouts of the trades he had been analyzing, though he knew she preferred working with digital data. "I've been following some strange market movements. Stock prices dropping and then bouncing back within minutes, wiping out small traders. I'm sure it's manipulation, but I need more than just gut instinct. I need to understand the mechanics behind it."

Maya skimmed the pages briefly, then gestured for him to hand over the USB drive with the raw data. "Let me guess, you want me to dig through the numbers and find out who's pulling the strings?"

"Exactly," Arjun replied. "There's something happening beneath the surface, and I think it's bigger than just a few rogue traders. I think it's coordinated."

Maya's eyes sparkled with interest. "Well, let's see what the data says."

The first step in Maya's process was to organize the data. Arjun had given her thousands of trades to sift through, each one a potential clue in the puzzle they were trying to solve. Maya's fingers flew over the keyboard as she loaded the information into her custom-built software, designed to detect anomalies in trading patterns.

Over the next few hours, she ran various algorithms, looking for patterns that the human eye couldn't see—spikes in trading volume, sudden shifts in stock prices, and unusual clusters of trades executed within milliseconds of each other.

As she worked, Arjun watched the screen, mesmerized by the complexity of the data. It was a world he didn't fully understand, but he knew that the answers were hidden somewhere in those numbers.

"I'm running an algorithmic analysis to detect coordinated trading activity," Maya explained, not taking her eyes off the screen. "If there's any manipulation happening, it will show up in the form of sudden spikes in volume, followed by sharp price movements. But the key is looking at the timing. If multiple trades happen at exactly the same time, it's not a coincidence. It's deliberate."

Arjun nodded, understanding just enough to follow along. He had always been good at piecing together narratives, but this was a different kind of story—a story told in numbers and algorithms.

After several hours, Maya leaned back in her chair, her expression thoughtful. "There's definitely something here," she said. "Look at this."

She pointed to a chart on the screen, where several spikes in trading volume were highlighted. Each spike was followed by a sharp drop in stock prices, just like the patterns Arjun had been seeing.

"These trades are happening within milliseconds of each other," Maya continued. "That's not normal. It's almost like someone is flooding the market with sell orders all at once, causing the price to crash. And then, just as quickly, the price bounces back. Whoever's behind this is using their capital to create an artificial panic."

Arjun felt a surge of excitement. "So it's real. It's not just my imagination."

"Oh, it's real," Maya said, her tone serious. "But here's the problem—it's nearly impossible to trace the source of these trades. The big players use multiple accounts, shell companies, and offshore brokers to hide their tracks. They're using high-frequency trading algorithms to execute these trades at lightning speed, making it almost impossible for regulators to catch them in the act."

Arjun leaned closer to the screen, studying the patterns Maya had uncovered. It was clear that the trades were coordinated, but they were happening across multiple exchanges and platforms, making it difficult to pinpoint exactly who was behind them.

Maya zoomed in on one particular stock that had experienced a dramatic drop followed by a rapid recovery. "Look at this," she said. "This stock fell by nearly 20% in less than a minute, wiping out anyone who was holding it. But if you look closely, the sell orders that caused the drop all came in at exactly the same time. That's not a natural market move. That's manipulation."

She clicked through several more examples, each one showing a similar pattern—sudden spikes in volume, followed by sharp price movements that seemed to defy logic.

"But here's the thing," Maya continued. "The people behind these trades aren't just making money on the way down. They're also profiting when the stock rebounds. It's a double-edged sword. They create the panic, force small traders to sell at a loss, and then buy up the shares at a discount. It's a win-win for them."

Arjun felt a knot of anger tighten in his chest. The more he learned about The Syndicate, the more he realized just how deeply they were embedded in the financial system. They weren't just manipulating the market for profit—they were rigging the entire game.

Maya continued her analysis, diving deeper into the data to uncover the full extent of the manipulation. What she found was even more disturbing than Arjun had imagined.

"These guys aren't just moving individual stocks," she said. "They're manipulating entire sectors. Look at this."

She pulled up a chart showing the trading activity in the tech sector over the past few months. The pattern was eerily similar to the individual stock movements—sudden spikes in volume,

THE SILENT HAND: BEHIND THE MARKET'S ILLUSION

followed by sharp drops in prices. But instead of just one or two stocks, the entire sector was being affected.

"They're creating the illusion of supply and demand," Maya explained. "By placing massive buy or sell orders, they can move the entire market in one direction or another. Small traders think they're reacting to real news or economic trends, but it's all an illusion. The Syndicate is controlling the narrative."

Arjun was stunned. He had suspected that the manipulation was widespread, but this was on a whole different level. The Syndicate wasn't just profiting from individual stocks—they were moving entire sectors, controlling the flow of money in and out of the market.

"And here's the kicker," Maya said, her voice tinged with frustration. "There's no way to stop it. The regulators are outmatched. The Syndicate has more money, more resources, and more access to technology than anyone else. They're playing a game that no one else can win."

As Maya continued to analyze the data, she uncovered another disturbing trend—the use of dark pools.

Dark pools were private exchanges where large institutional investors could trade stocks without revealing their intentions to the public. These exchanges were designed to provide anonymity, allowing big players to move large volumes of shares without affecting the market price. But as Maya dug deeper, she realized that The Syndicate was using dark pools to hide their trades from regulators and the public.

"They're hiding in plain sight," Maya said, shaking her head. "By using dark pools, they can execute massive trades without anyone knowing. It's the perfect way to manipulate the market without leaving a trace."

Arjun felt a sinking feeling in his stomach. The more he learned, the more he realized just how formidable The Syndicate was. They had created a system that was nearly impossible to penetrate, using technology, money, and influence to control the market from the shadows.

But Maya wasn't done yet. She had one more revelation that would change everything.

"There's one more thing I found," she said, pulling up a final chart. "This pattern shows up in every stock I've analyzed, across multiple sectors. It's not just The Syndicate—it's an entire network of traders, brokers, and institutions, all working together to manipulate the market."

She paused, letting the weight of her words sink in. "It's bigger than we thought, Arjun. The Syndicate is just the tip of the iceberg. There's a whole system in place, designed to trap small traders and funnel money into the hands of the few."

Arjun sat in silence, processing everything he had just learned. The Syndicate was real, but they were part of a much larger machine. A machine that had been rigging the stock market for years, perhaps even decades.

He looked at Maya, his mind racing with questions. "What do we do now?"

Maya leaned back in her chair, her expression serious. "We keep digging. We need more evidence—something concrete that we can take to the public. But we have to be careful. If The Syndicate finds out what we're doing, they'll come after us."

Arjun nodded, knowing that the road ahead would be dangerous. But he was more determined than ever to expose the truth. The market was a battlefield, and small traders were the casualties. It was time to level the playing field.

As he left Maya's office, he felt a renewed sense of purpose. The numbers didn't lie. There were echoes in the data—echoes of a conspiracy that reached the highest levels of power. And Arjun was going to bring it all crashing down.

Chapter 4: "Smoke and Mirrors"

Arjun's investigation was starting to unearth secrets that ran deeper than he had ever anticipated. After weeks of pouring through trading data and interviewing insiders, he had uncovered a sophisticated web of market manipulation orchestrated by The Syndicate. But now, his investigation was about to take a darker turn.

This wasn't just a matter of financial crimes or high-frequency traders pulling strings. The tentacles of The Syndicate reached into the corridors of political power. As Arjun followed the money, he began to realize that the market manipulation he had uncovered was not just a financial operation—it was a political one.

The first clue came when Arjun received an anonymous tip from a source within the Ministry of Finance. The message was cryptic but intriguing: *"Look into the bills proposed in Parliament. Some laws were made for the stock market, not the people."*

It was a bold accusation, and Arjun knew that if true, it would expose a staggering level of corruption. For years, people had suspected that politicians were using their influence for personal gain, but proving it was another matter. The idea that laws were being written to manipulate the market went beyond anything Arjun had imagined. But now, with this lead, he had a direction.

The first step was to gather more information. Arjun spent days combing through the legislative archives, looking for patterns in the bills that had been passed over the last few years. It wasn't enough to find a single law that seemed suspicious; he needed to find a connection between political actions and the market movements he had already identified.

It didn't take long for a pattern to emerge.

Several bills that had been pushed through Parliament—bills that barely made headlines—were directly tied to industries that had seen massive, sudden fluctuations in stock prices. These bills, often framed as "economic reforms" or "investment incentives," seemed innocuous on the surface. They claimed to open up industries to more foreign direct investment, reduce regulatory burdens, or streamline tax policies. But the real beneficiaries were not the public or the economy; they were the insiders who knew the exact timing of the changes.

Arjun's pulse quickened as he began connecting the dots. He found that key stocks in industries like pharmaceuticals, infrastructure, and technology had surged in value right after the announcement of these new policies, only to crash shortly after. It was as if someone had known exactly when to get in and out of these stocks. And that someone, Arjun suspected, had access to insider information from the highest levels of government.

The breakthrough came when Arjun met with a former government official who had worked in the Ministry of Finance. The official, who insisted on anonymity, confirmed Arjun's suspicions. The man revealed that several politicians were in league with The Syndicate, using their positions to pass laws that would benefit their financial interests. These laws were often buried in complex legislative packages, carefully crafted to appear beneficial to the public but were, in reality, designed to manipulate stock prices.

The official handed Arjun a thick envelope. Inside was a confidential document—a report from an internal government audit that had never been made public. The report detailed a series of suspicious trades made by high-ranking officials just days before key legislation was passed.

"This is just the tip of the iceberg," the former official said, his voice tinged with bitterness. "The Syndicate has infiltrated the highest levels of government. They're not just using the market to get rich—they're using the government itself to control it."

Arjun felt a chill run down his spine as he read through the document. The names listed in the report were some of the most powerful figures in the country—members of Parliament, cabinet ministers, and even advisors to the Prime Minister. The report detailed how these individuals had used insider knowledge to buy and sell stocks at just the right moment, making millions in the process.

One particular section of the document caught Arjun's eye. It described a series of bills related to the pharmaceutical industry. In the weeks leading up to the passage of these bills, stocks in several major pharmaceutical companies had spiked dramatically. The insiders had bought shares before the announcement, riding the wave of optimism that followed. But as soon as the bills passed, and the stocks hit their peak, they had dumped their shares, leaving small investors to bear the losses when the prices inevitably crashed.

Arjun realized that this was how The Syndicate operated—they created illusions of prosperity, pushing stocks to artificial highs before pulling the rug out from under unsuspecting investors. And they did it with the full cooperation of those in power.

As Arjun dug deeper into the political connections, he began to uncover the mechanics of how these back-channel deals were made. Through a series of off-the-record interviews with insiders and former aides, he learned that the key figures in The Syndicate had direct lines of communication with top politicians. They met in private, away from prying eyes, often under the guise of charity events, exclusive parties, or informal gatherings at luxury resorts.

It was in these secretive meetings that the real decisions were made. Politicians would offer insider information—details about upcoming bills, regulatory changes, or government contracts—in exchange for financial kickbacks or future favors. The Syndicate, in turn, would use this information to manipulate the market, profiting from the artificially inflated stock prices.

The deals were discreet, carefully orchestrated to avoid detection. Money would flow through offshore accounts, shell companies, and intermediaries, making it nearly impossible to trace. But Arjun knew that if he could follow the money trail, he might be able to expose the entire operation.

One of his sources, a former aide to a powerful politician, described how the system worked. "It's all about timing," the aide explained. "They pass a bill that benefits a certain industry—let's say infrastructure. They let The Syndicate know in advance, and The Syndicate buys up shares in the companies that will benefit. Once the stock prices rise, they sell, making millions in the process. It's a win-win. The politicians get their kickbacks, and The Syndicate gets richer."

Arjun was beginning to understand just how deep the corruption ran. The stock market wasn't just a playground for the rich—it was a tool for those in power to manipulate for their own gain.

Arjun's investigation was now reaching its most dangerous phase. He had uncovered enough evidence to prove that key figures in the Ministry of Finance and Parliament were in cahoots with The Syndicate. But he knew that exposing this level of corruption would come at a price.

As he worked late into the night, piecing together his findings, Arjun couldn't shake the feeling that he was being watched. He had already received several anonymous threats warning him to stop his investigation, but he couldn't back down now. He was too close to the truth.

One name kept coming up in his investigation—a shadowy figure known only as "The Puppet Master." According to his sources, this individual was the true leader of The Syndicate, the one pulling the strings behind the scenes. The Puppet Master wasn't a politician or a financier—he was something far more dangerous. He was a kingmaker, someone who had the power to make or break careers in both the financial and political worlds.

Arjun knew that if he could find The Puppet Master, he would finally be able to expose the entire operation. But finding this elusive figure was easier said than done. The Puppet Master operated in the shadows, rarely showing his face in public. Even those within The Syndicate didn't know his true identity.

But Arjun had a lead.

One of his contacts, a former lobbyist who had worked closely with The Syndicate, claimed to have met The Puppet Master once, at a private gathering of elite financiers and politicians. The lobbyist described him as a man of few words, but with an air of authority that commanded respect. He was the one who decided which laws would be passed, which stocks would rise and fall, and who would profit from the manipulation.

"He's the real power behind the throne," the lobbyist had said. "If you can expose him, you'll bring the whole house of cards crashing down."

With this new information, Arjun began to connect the dots. The Syndicate wasn't just manipulating the stock market for financial gain—they were shaping the entire political landscape. They had the power to influence elections, pass laws, and control the flow of money in and out of the country. And they did it all under the guise of economic growth and free markets.

The confidential document Arjun had obtained was just the beginning. He now had evidence that several bills proposed in

Parliament were deliberately designed to benefit certain industries, driving up stock prices right before The Syndicate dumped their shares. It was a classic pump-and-dump scheme, but on a massive scale, orchestrated at the highest levels of power.

Arjun knew that exposing this conspiracy would be dangerous. The Syndicate had already proven that they would stop at nothing to protect their interests. But he also knew that the public deserved to know the truth.

As he prepared to publish his findings, Arjun felt a sense of both dread and determination. The smoke and mirrors that had kept The Syndicate's operation hidden for so long were about to be shattered. The truth was finally coming to light.

But at what cost?

In the days leading up to the publication of his exposé, Arjun was on edge. He had taken every precaution to ensure that his story would reach the public without interference. He had encrypted his files, stored backups in multiple locations, and even sent copies of his report to trusted colleagues in case something happened to him.

But as the day approached, the threats intensified. Anonymous phone calls, cryptic messages, and strange cars parked outside his apartment—all signs that The Syndicate was watching his every move.

Arjun knew that once the story broke, there would be no turning back. The powerful figures he had exposed would come after him with everything they had. But he was ready. The market wasn't free, and neither was the government. It was time to tear down the façade and show the world the truth.

The calm before the storm was over. The storm itself was about to begin.

The deeper Arjun delved into his investigation, the more he realized that The Syndicate's influence stretched far beyond just the corridors of power and the backrooms of finance. The true extent of their operation was far more insidious. Their control over the stock market wasn't limited to back-channel deals or secret trades—it extended into the very fabric of public perception itself. And nowhere was this more apparent than in the financial media.

Arjun had always known that the media played a role in shaping market sentiment. Financial news outlets provided constant streams of information, commentary, and analysis that traders and investors relied on to make decisions. A positive or negative spin on a stock could lead to wild fluctuations in its price. But what Arjun hadn't fully grasped until now was just how deeply some elements of the financial media were intertwined with the manipulation he had uncovered.

It wasn't just about presenting the news—it was about creating the news. And in doing so, The Syndicate had weaponized the media as a tool for their own gain, pushing narratives that fueled market movements they could profit from.

The first time Arjun truly noticed the media's role in market manipulation was during a sudden, inexplicable market rally in the technology sector. Over the course of just a few days, stock prices for several tech companies had soared, driven by a flurry of optimistic reports from various financial news outlets. Headlines touted these companies as the "next big thing," and analysts appeared on television, giving glowing reviews of their future prospects.

But Arjun, having already begun his investigation into The Syndicate, saw something else. He had access to trading data that showed significant activity by hedge funds connected to The Syndicate. These funds had been quietly accumulating shares in these tech companies for weeks, long before the media hype began. When the prices shot up, they began selling off their holdings, cashing in on the artificial surge in demand driven by small traders and retail investors who had bought into the hype.

It was a classic pump-and-dump scheme, but this time, the pump wasn't coming from shady stock promoters on the internet—it was coming from respected journalists and analysts on national television.

Arjun's suspicions grew. He started paying closer attention to the timing of media coverage and how it aligned with market movements. It wasn't long before he noticed a pattern. Stocks would rise or fall sharply after being featured prominently in the financial news. The media was creating waves of optimism or fear, and small traders were being caught in the undertow.

But who was pulling the strings behind these carefully orchestrated media campaigns?

Arjun had his answer sooner than expected. One evening, while watching a popular financial news show, he noticed something peculiar. The host, an influential on-air personality named Dev Sharma, was discussing a recent selloff in the pharmaceutical sector. Dev was known for his confident, authoritative demeanor and was considered a reliable voice in the financial world. His predictions were often treated as gospel by retail traders and smaller investors.

On this particular episode, Dev was talking about a specific pharmaceutical company that had seen its stock price drop sharply over the past few days. He made the case that the selloff was overblown, citing "inside sources" who assured him that the company's fundamentals were strong and that a rebound was imminent.

The next day, the stock did indeed rebound, just as Dev had predicted. Small traders, eager to capitalize on the opportunity, piled in. But Arjun, with his knowledge of The Syndicate's tactics, wasn't so easily convinced. He dug into the trading data and found something alarming. Hedge funds with ties to The Syndicate had been buying up shares of the company in question just hours before Dev's segment aired. They had bought low, knowing that the media coverage would cause the price to rise, and were now sitting on significant profits.

This wasn't just coincidence. The timing was too perfect. It was clear that Dev Sharma wasn't just an impartial journalist—he was part of the game. He was using his platform to influence the market in ways that benefited The Syndicate.

Arjun began researching Dev's background, looking for any connections to the world of finance. What he found only confirmed his suspicions. Dev had once worked as an analyst at a major hedge fund, one that Arjun had already linked to The Syndicate. Though he had left that world behind to pursue a career in journalism, it was clear that his ties to the financial elite had never been severed.

The more Arjun looked into the role of the media in market manipulation, the more he realized just how deeply entrenched the problem was. It wasn't just Dev Sharma. Across the board, influential financial commentators and analysts were working hand in glove with powerful hedge funds and investment banks, using their platforms to push narratives that aligned with the interests of The Syndicate.

Arjun began reaching out to contacts within the media industry, hoping to find someone willing to talk. After several dead ends, he finally found a source—an editor at a prominent financial news outlet who had become disillusioned with the industry's direction.

The editor, speaking on the condition of anonymity, confirmed Arjun's worst fears. The financial media was being used as a tool to manipulate the market. Journalists and analysts were regularly given "tips" by hedge funds and investment banks—tips that were designed to create hype or fear around specific stocks. In exchange, these media personalities were given exclusive access to inside information or rewarded with lucrative speaking engagements and consulting gigs.

"It's all about influence," the editor said. "The Syndicate knows that retail traders trust these analysts and journalists. They rely on them for advice. So, when someone like Dev Sharma goes on TV and says a stock is going to skyrocket, people believe him. They don't realize that he's just a mouthpiece for The Syndicate."

Arjun was stunned. He had always known that the media played a role in shaping market sentiment, but he hadn't realized just how direct the manipulation was. The financial news wasn't just reporting on the market—it was actively shaping it.

Arjun began to focus on the two primary emotions that moved markets: greed and fear. The financial media, under the influence of The Syndicate, knew exactly how to exploit these emotions to their advantage. It was a delicate balancing act—too much greed, and the market would become overheated; too much fear, and it would crash. The goal was to create just the right amount of hype or panic to trigger the desired market moves.

Arjun recalled a recent case involving a tech startup that had been hyped by the media as the next "unicorn"—a company that would revolutionize its industry and generate massive profits for early investors. For weeks, financial news outlets ran glowing profiles of the company's founder, highlighting its cutting-edge technology and innovative business model. Analysts on television gushed about its potential, urging viewers to buy in before the stock soared.

Retail investors, eager to cash in on the next big thing, rushed to buy shares. The stock price surged, hitting record highs within days of the media blitz. But Arjun had been watching closely, and he saw the telltale signs of manipulation. The hedge funds linked to The Syndicate had been accumulating shares long before the media hype began. And once the stock reached its peak, they started selling, pocketing millions in profits.

It didn't take long for the truth to come out. The company's technology wasn't as revolutionary as claimed, and its business model was deeply flawed. The stock price plummeted, wiping out the savings of countless small investors who had bought into the media-driven hype.

This was how The Syndicate operated. They used the media to create illusions—of success, of failure, of opportunity. And they reaped the rewards while small traders were left holding the bag.

As Arjun dug deeper, he began to uncover the financial connections that linked media personalities like Dev Sharma to the hedge funds and investment banks involved in the manipulation. These ties weren't always obvious, but they were there, hidden behind layers of shell companies, consulting contracts, and offshore accounts.

One of the most glaring examples came when Arjun discovered that several high-profile analysts, who regularly appeared on television to discuss the stock market, were also quietly working as consultants for hedge funds tied to The Syndicate. These analysts were being paid hefty fees to provide "insights" that conveniently aligned with the trading strategies of the funds they were advising.

It was a blatant conflict of interest, but it was happening in plain sight. The public had no idea that the analysts they trusted for impartial advice were being paid to push narratives that benefited a select group of elite financiers.

Arjun began to focus on one particular hedge fund—Riverton Capital, a fund he had already linked to The Syndicate. He discovered that Riverton had been a major client of Dev Sharma's consulting firm, paying him millions over the years for his "expertise." At the same time, Dev had been using his platform on television to talk up stocks that Riverton was investing in, creating artificial demand and driving up prices.

It was a perfect symbiotic relationship. The hedge fund made money, the media personality gained influence, and The Syndicate continued to manipulate the market with impunity.

What disturbed Arjun the most was the erosion of public trust. Small traders and retail investors relied on the media for information and guidance. They turned to financial news outlets, analysts, and commentators to make sense of the market's complexities. But the very institutions they trusted were working against them, pushing narratives designed to line the pockets of the wealthy and powerful.

Arjun realized that this was perhaps the most dangerous aspect of The Syndicate's operation. They had not only corrupted the market—they had corrupted the very sources of information that people relied on to navigate it.

As he sat at his desk, reviewing the mountain of evidence he had gathered, Arjun knew that exposing The Syndicate's control over the media would be the key to bringing them down. The public needed to see the truth—that the financial news they consumed wasn't impartial, that the analysts they trusted weren't acting in their best interests.

The media was supposed to be the watchdog, holding the powerful accountable. But in the case of The Syndicate, it had become something else entirely—a weapon used to manipulate the masses and enrich the few.

With the media now firmly in his sights, Arjun prepared to take the next step in his investigation. He knew that going after someone as influential as Dev Sharma would be risky. Dev had powerful friends, and The Syndicate wouldn't hesitate to retaliate if they felt threatened.

But Arjun also knew that the media was the linchpin of The Syndicate's operation. If he could expose their control over the narrative, he could begin to unravel the entire scheme.

It wouldn't be easy. The Syndicate had spent years building their media mirage, creating an illusion of transparency and trust. But Arjun was determined to break through the smoke and mirrors.

The truth was out there, hidden beneath layers of deception. And Arjun was going to find it, no matter the cost.

Chapter 6: "The Shark Tank"

Arjun and Maya sat in a dimly lit café tucked away in one of Mumbai's quieter neighborhoods. The late afternoon sun filtered through the worn blinds, casting long shadows over the table. Across from them sat Vikram Malhotra, a retired stockbroker who once thrived in the high-stakes world of finance. His grizzled appearance and furrowed brow reflected the weight of his past—a past he was now prepared to unburden, and one that Arjun and Maya hoped would shed light on the intricacies of The Syndicate's inner workings.

Vikram had agreed to speak with them under one condition: absolute confidentiality. Having left the game years ago, he still lived in fear of retribution from powerful players who had no qualms about silencing those who betrayed their secrets. But Vikram had grown tired of the guilt that weighed him down. He wanted redemption, a chance to make things right. And so, he began to speak, his voice steady yet laden with the gravity of what he was about to reveal.

"The stock market," Vikram began, his voice hoarse, "isn't just a place where buyers and sellers meet to trade. For most people, it's a game of numbers, of logic, and of trends. But for the people at the top—the real players—it's a battlefield. A game of power. And the weapons? Capital. Massive amounts of capital."

Arjun and Maya listened intently, leaning forward as Vikram continued.

"You see, when you're dealing with billions, you can move markets. A single trade from a hedge fund or institutional investor can send ripples through the entire market, causing prices to shift dramatically. But it's not just about buying and selling stocks. It's much more complex than that. The real game is played with derivatives—options, futures, indices. These instruments allow you to control vast sums of money with relatively little capital. And that's where the manipulation happens."

Vikram paused for a moment, sipping his tea before continuing. "The Syndicate mastered this game. They could create violent market moves with ease, using options and futures to leverage their positions. They didn't need to buy up entire companies to move the market—they just needed to control the perception of where the market was going. And once they did that, they could push prices in any direction they wanted."

Maya, always curious about the technical aspects of the market, interjected. "But how do they do it? How do they use options and futures to manipulate the market so effectively?"

Vikram nodded, as if expecting the question. "It starts with setting the stage. The Syndicate would first decide which stock, index, or sector they wanted to manipulate. Let's say, for example, they wanted to push the price of a tech stock up. They'd quietly accumulate call options—contracts that give the buyer the right to purchase the stock at a set price within a certain time frame. These options require far less capital than buying the stock outright, but they allow you to control large amounts of shares. Once they had their options in place, they'd start moving the market."

"How?" Maya asked, her brow furrowed in concentration.

"By creating demand. They would start buying up shares in small increments, pushing the price up gradually. At the same time, they'd feed rumors to the financial media or analysts—stories about how the company was poised for explosive growth or had some groundbreaking technology in the pipeline. Retail investors, small traders, they'd see the stock rising, hear the positive news, and start piling in. It's called FOMO—the fear of missing out. People would jump in, pushing the price even higher."

Arjun's mind raced as he connected the dots. This was exactly what he had seen in the tech stock rally he had investigated earlier—the orchestrated rise, the media hype, the retail traders getting sucked in.

"And then," Vikram continued, "once the price had been driven up high enough, The Syndicate would start unloading their call options, pocketing huge profits. They'd exit just before the hype died down, leaving small traders holding the bag when the stock inevitably corrected."

"But it's not just about driving prices up," Vikram said, leaning in closer. "The Syndicate could crash markets just as easily as they could pump them up. And they did it all the time—especially when they wanted to shake out small traders or scoop up shares at a discount."

Maya's eyes widened. "You mean they engineered price crashes on purpose?"

"Absolutely," Vikram replied. "They'd use the same tactics, but in reverse. They'd accumulate put options—contracts that give the buyer the right to sell shares at a set price—quietly, over time. Then, they'd start selling off small chunks of stock, just enough to create the impression that the market was turning bearish. Once the selling started, they'd feed rumors of bad news into the media—claims that a company's earnings would miss expectations, or that there was some regulatory trouble on the horizon."

"Fear is a powerful motivator," Vikram continued. "Once retail investors got spooked, the selling would accelerate. People would panic, thinking they were about to lose their savings, and they'd sell everything. The price would crash, and The Syndicate would profit from their put options."

Maya shook her head in disbelief. "But wouldn't regulators catch on to this? Wouldn't they notice these sudden crashes and investigate?"

Vikram chuckled darkly. "The beauty of it is that the markets are chaotic by nature. Prices go up and down all the time. A sudden drop in price isn't unusual, especially if it's accompanied by negative news. Regulators look for clear signs of manipulation—like coordinated trading or insider information. But The Syndicate was smart. They worked through proxies, shell companies, and offshore accounts. Their trades were scattered across different exchanges and timed to avoid detection. By the time regulators noticed anything suspicious, The Syndicate had already cashed out and moved on to the next target."

As Vikram spoke, Arjun couldn't help but think of the countless small traders who had been caught in The Syndicate's web. People who had worked hard, saved diligently, and invested their money in the hopes of building a better future—only to see their savings wiped out in a matter of hours by forces they couldn't even begin to understand.

"They never had a chance," Vikram said quietly, as if reading Arjun's thoughts. "The small traders, the retail investors—they were the cannon fodder in this game. The Syndicate didn't just profit from market moves—they profited from fear, from hope, from the emotions of everyday people who didn't know any better."

He recounted stories of traders who had been lured into the market by promises of quick riches, only to lose everything when the market turned against them. Vikram described how the manipulation was so subtle, so well-orchestrated, that most traders didn't even realize what had happened until it was too late.

"I remember one trader," Vikram said, his voice tinged with regret. "A young guy, just out of college. He had saved up for years, working odd jobs to put together a little nest egg. He started trading during one of the market booms, thinking he could turn a quick profit. But he got caught in one of The Syndicate's crashes. He lost everything—wiped out in a single day."

Vikram paused, his eyes downcast. "I saw it happen again and again. The Syndicate would push the market up, lure in the small traders, and then pull the rug out from under them. It was brutal. But that's how the game was played."

One of the most effective tools in The Syndicate's arsenal, Vikram explained, was the use of rumors and disinformation. In the fast-paced world of finance, information was everything. A single rumor could send a stock soaring—or crashing—within minutes. And The Syndicate had perfected the art of spreading rumors to manipulate the market to their advantage.

"They had people everywhere," Vikram said, his voice low. "In the media, in the banks, even in the regulatory agencies. They'd plant stories about companies—sometimes positive, sometimes negative—and then watch as the market reacted. It didn't matter if the stories were true or not. All that mattered was how the market responded."

He described how The Syndicate would often leak fake news about a company's earnings or its future prospects. Sometimes they'd spread rumors of a merger or acquisition to drive up the price of a stock. Other times, they'd hint at regulatory trouble or a pending lawsuit to drive the price down. The goal was always the same—to create volatility, to move the market in ways that they could profit from.

"And the thing is," Vikram said, "most of the time, the rumors were so plausible that people didn't question them. If a company's stock had been underperforming for a while, a rumor about bad earnings seemed believable. If a company was doing well, a story about a potential acquisition seemed reasonable. The Syndicate knew exactly how to play on people's expectations and fears."

Maya nodded, absorbing the weight of what Vikram was saying. "So they weren't just manipulating the market—they were manipulating people's perceptions of the market."

"Exactly," Vikram replied. "It was all about creating illusions—making people believe that a stock was worth more or less than it really was. And in the chaos, The Syndicate would quietly make their moves, profiting while everyone else was caught up in the frenzy."

By the end of their conversation, Arjun and Maya felt as though they had been given a glimpse into a world few outsiders ever saw. The stock market was not the level playing field it appeared to be. It was a shark tank, where the biggest predators thrived by preying on the weak. And The Syndicate was the biggest predator of them all.

Vikram looked at them with a mixture of relief and resignation. He had unburdened himself, but in doing so, he had also exposed himself to danger.

"You have to be careful," he warned. "The Syndicate doesn't take kindly to people who try to expose them. If they find out you're investigating them, they'll come after you."

Arjun nodded, fully aware of the risks. But he also knew that they were closer than ever to uncovering the full extent of The Syndicate's operation. They had the pieces of the puzzle. Now it was a matter of putting them together.

As they left the café, Arjun and Maya exchanged a silent look of determination. The more they uncovered, the more dangerous the investigation became. But they couldn't turn back now. The truth was within reach, and they were going to expose it—no matter the cost.

The Syndicate had operated in the shadows for too long, using the stock market as their personal playground while leaving a trail of broken lives in their wake. But Arjun and Maya were determined to shine a light on the darkness. The game was far from over, but for the first time, they had the upper hand.

And as they walked away from the café, they knew one thing for certain: the sharks were circling, but they were ready to fight back.

Chapter 7: "The Secret Ledger"

Arjun sat in his apartment, staring at the small, unremarkable brown envelope that had appeared on his doorstep. It looked ordinary—nothing about it indicated the explosive contents inside. Yet, deep down, Arjun knew that this envelope would change everything. Inside it was The Syndicate's secret ledger, the key to unraveling a conspiracy that went far beyond the stock market. The person who had dropped it off had vanished without a trace, leaving Arjun with more questions than answers.

As he cautiously opened the envelope, his hands trembled with a mix of excitement and dread. The world of finance was murky enough, but this ledger, if it was what he thought it was, would confirm suspicions of something far more insidious—an intricate web of corruption, black money, and power that stretched from the highest echelons of politics and media down to the very brokers who manipulated the markets. This wasn't just about stock market manipulation anymore. It was about the very integrity of the nation's financial system and its political institutions.

The ledger was thick, filled with pages of cryptic codes, financial jargon, and complex transaction histories. At first glance, it looked like any other business document—columns of numbers, transaction dates, account names—but upon closer inspection, Arjun realized that this was no ordinary financial record. Each transaction had ties to off-shore shell companies, untraceable accounts, and faceless entities that had been designed to hide their true origin.

The first entry Arjun focused on was dated about three years ago, a large transfer from a company he had never heard of—"Deltanex Holdings." A quick online search revealed that it was a shell corporation registered in the Cayman Islands, known for its lax financial regulations. The amount transferred was staggering: over ₹500 crore, moved in a series of small, calculated installments designed to avoid raising red flags. From Deltanex, the money had been funneled into several smaller accounts, all tied to various players in the stock market.

But what really caught Arjun's attention was not the money itself, but the purpose behind these trades. Next to each transaction was a note—cryptic phrases like "P. Gupta - Media Influence," "IPO pump strategy," and "Pre-election boost." These weren't just financial trades; they were coordinated attacks on the market, designed to influence stock prices for political or personal gain. And the people behind them? Names Arjun recognized all too well.

As Arjun delved deeper into the ledger, the names started appearing. At first, they were just initials—"P.G.", "R.K.", "S.P."—but the accompanying details made it clear who these people were. The ledger laid out a system of kickbacks and bribes that tied The Syndicate to some of the most powerful figures in the country. Politicians, bureaucrats, and senior government officials were all on the take, their hands greased by the illegal flows of money orchestrated by The Syndicate.

One particular entry sent a chill down Arjun's spine. It referenced a high-ranking official in the Ministry of Finance. The note next to his name read: "Budget leak - ₹10 crore." Arjun's pulse quickened. This wasn't just market manipulation anymore. This was financial sabotage at the national level. The Syndicate had paid a bribe to obtain insider information about the country's upcoming budget, allowing them to strategically place trades in anticipation of policy changes. Billions could be made with the right kind of knowledge, and The Syndicate had bought it at the source.

But it wasn't just the financial world that had been corrupted. The ledger listed political donations to prominent figures in key constituencies ahead of elections, funneling black money into campaigns in exchange for favorable policies. Politicians who publicly championed clean governance and economic reform were secretly on The Syndicate's payroll, ensuring that their illegal schemes went unchecked.

Arjun felt a wave of anger wash over him as he connected the dots. These were the same politicians who had campaigned on promises of transparency and integrity, yet they were nothing more than puppets, controlled by The Syndicate's dirty money. Worse still, these were the people who held the fate of the nation in their hands—passing laws, influencing markets, and shaping the economy. They were supposed to protect the country, but they were selling it out for personal gain.

The more Arjun examined the ledger, the more intricate and shocking the web of corruption became. It wasn't just politicians and bureaucrats who were involved. The media, which had always positioned itself as the watchdog of democracy, was equally compromised.

Next to many of the large transactions were the names of well-known journalists and media executives. Arjun's stomach churned as he read the familiar names—anchors and commentators who had made a career out of shaping public opinion, some of whom had even helped launch his own investigative career. These same people were listed as receiving payouts from The Syndicate. The amounts varied—some were small, as if to keep them on a retainer, while others were huge, possibly in exchange for bigger favors.

One entry stood out: "S.B. - ₹50 lakh - IPO pump coverage." Arjun recognized the initials as belonging to a high-profile news anchor who was often seen commenting on the stock market. The note next to the entry indicated that this anchor had been paid to provide favorable coverage of a particular IPO, hyping it up to retail investors and creating a buying frenzy. The stock, of course, had later crashed, leaving small investors ruined. But by then, The Syndicate had already made their money and pulled out.

Arjun felt sick. He had long suspected that certain members of the media were complicit in market manipulation, but this was concrete proof. These journalists weren't just reporting the news—they were shaping it, manipulating public opinion to serve the interests of the wealthy elite. The very institutions that people trusted to inform them were nothing more than tools in The Syndicate's hands.

The ledger was a map of illicit financial flows, and as Arjun continued to piece together the puzzle, he realized how deeply The Syndicate had embedded itself into the fabric of the financial system. At the heart of their operation were the shell companies—offshore entities designed to hide the origin of funds and make them appear legitimate.

Each of these shell companies acted as a buffer, insulating The Syndicate from direct involvement in the trades. Deltanex Holdings was just one of many. The ledger listed dozens of similar entities, each registered in tax havens like the British Virgin Islands, Panama, and the Isle of Man. These companies existed solely on paper, with no real operations or employees. Their sole purpose was to move money around without attracting attention.

Arjun was no stranger to the concept of black money—unaccounted-for income that was funneled into offshore accounts to avoid taxes. But seeing it laid out so clearly in the ledger was staggering. Billions of rupees had flowed in and out of these shell companies, funding market manipulation, political corruption, and media payoffs. The money itself was impossible to trace, but the effects were all too real. The Syndicate was siphoning off the wealth of the nation, using illegal funds to enrich themselves at the expense of ordinary citizens.

One transaction in particular caught Arjun's eye. It was a large transfer from a company called "Altezza Ventures" to an account in Singapore. The amount was staggering—₹1,000 crore, moved in a series of small transactions over the course of a month. The note next to the transfer read: "Election fund - North Zone." This wasn't just market manipulation. This was political interference on a massive scale. The Syndicate wasn't just rigging stock prices—they were buying elections, ensuring that their chosen candidates would hold power and protect their interests.

As Arjun pored over the ledger, the full scope of The Syndicate's operation came into focus. This was a conspiracy that touched every corner of society—politics, finance, media, and beyond. The Syndicate had infiltrated the very institutions that were supposed to protect the public, using their influence to rig the game in their favor.

But with this realization came a growing sense of fear. The people listed in this ledger were powerful—more powerful than Arjun had ever imagined. And now that he had the ledger, he was a threat to them. If they found out that he had this information, they wouldn't hesitate to silence him.

Arjun knew he couldn't go to the authorities—not yet. The ledger implicated too many high-ranking officials, and he couldn't trust that the police or the regulators weren't already in The Syndicate's pocket. He needed to be careful, to gather more evidence and find a way to expose this corruption without getting himself killed in the process.

Arjun decided to call Maya. She had been his partner in this investigation from the beginning, and he trusted her implicitly. When she arrived at his apartment, he showed her the ledger.

Maya's face paled as she flipped through the pages. "This is...this is huge," she whispered. "This goes all the way to the top."

Arjun nodded. "We have to be careful. If The Syndicate finds out we have this, they'll come after us."

Maya looked up from the ledger, her eyes wide with fear and determination. "We can't keep this to ourselves. People need to know the truth."

"I know," Arjun replied. "But we need to be smart about how we do it. We can't trust anyone right now—not the police, not the media, not even the government. We have to find a way to expose this without getting ourselves killed."

Maya closed the ledger and looked at Arjun. "We're in deep now. But we can't stop. We're too close."

Arjun nodded. They had come too far to turn back now. The ledger was the key to taking down The Syndicate, but it was also a death sentence if they weren't careful. They would need to plan their next move carefully, and they would need allies—people they could trust.

With the ledger in their possession, Arjun and Maya had the evidence they needed to take down The Syndicate. But they also knew that they were in more danger than ever before. The people listed in the ledger wouldn't hesitate to eliminate anyone who threatened their empire.

As they sat in Arjun's apartment, planning their next steps, they knew that the road ahead would be treacherous. The Syndicate was a powerful and dangerous enemy, but they weren't invincible. Arjun and Maya had something they didn't—the truth. And they were going to use it to bring The Syndicate down, no matter the cost.

But as they prepared to go to war with one of the most powerful criminal organizations in the country, they knew that the real battle was just beginning. The sharks were circling, and it was only a matter of time before they struck.

Chapter 8: "A Wolf in the Shadows"

The atmosphere in Arjun's apartment had shifted since the discovery of the ledger. Where once there had been cautious optimism, now there was a looming sense of dread. The Syndicate had become more than just a financial conspiracy—its tendrils reached into the darkest corners of society, and Arjun knew they wouldn't stand idly by while he worked to expose them. Still, nothing had prepared him for how personal the battle was about to become.

It started subtly. Arjun noticed someone following him. At first, he thought it was just paranoia. After all, his mind was constantly on high alert after uncovering the Syndicate's secret ledger. Every shadow seemed longer, every passing glance felt laden with suspicion. But when the same black sedan appeared on three separate occasions, parked just down the street from his apartment and later outside the café where he met Maya, he knew something was wrong.

Maya had grown more concerned, too. She had always been the one to reassure Arjun when things seemed to be spiraling out of control. But when her computer was hacked and all her research files disappeared, even she couldn't keep the fear out of her voice. It wasn't just her work that had been breached; personal messages, financial details, and even photos from her private life had been accessed. Someone was sending a message.

They were no longer dealing with faceless corporate greed. The Syndicate had made it clear that they could reach into Arjun's and Maya's lives whenever they wanted.

The situation escalated quickly after the hacking incident. Harassment took on new forms. Arjun began receiving ominous phone calls—always from blocked numbers, always silent on the other end. Sometimes the calls would come in the middle of the night, waking him up from restless sleep, as if to remind him that they were always watching. His emails were bombarded with strange messages—some offering bribes in exchange for silence, others making thinly veiled threats about what would happen if he didn't stop digging.

One evening, after a particularly exhausting day of research, Arjun returned home to find his apartment door slightly ajar. His heart raced as he stepped inside, scanning the room for signs of an intruder. Nothing seemed out of place at first glance, but then he noticed a single sheet of paper on the kitchen counter. It was blank, save for a message scrawled in bold, black letters: "Stop now, or there will be consequences."

Arjun knew it wasn't an empty threat. The Syndicate had gone from passive intimidation to active warning. They were flexing their muscles, showing him just how close they could get. And if he didn't back off, the next step would be much worse.

For Maya, the situation was equally frightening. After her data was hacked, she tried to regain control of her accounts, but every attempt was met with failure. Passwords were reset before she could act, and personal files were locked away from her. Even more troubling, her social media accounts began posting strange, inflammatory messages—things she would never say, designed to discredit her reputation and cast doubt on her credibility as a journalist. Colleagues reached out, confused by the posts, and she had to scramble to explain that her accounts had been compromised.

One evening, as she was leaving her office, Maya noticed a man watching her from across the street. He was tall, with a thick coat and a cap pulled low over his eyes. At first, she thought he might just be a passerby, but when she took a few steps toward her car, he started following her. She quickened her pace, her heart pounding in her chest, but so did he.

Panicking, she ducked into a nearby coffee shop, hoping the presence of other people would deter him. The man stopped outside for a moment, staring at her through the glass window. Maya's hands shook as she pretended to look at her phone, trying to act like everything was normal. After what felt like an eternity, the man turned and walked away, but Maya knew this wouldn't be the last time.

When she called Arjun later that night, her voice was strained with fear. "They're following me, Arjun. I'm sure of it. We need to be careful—really careful."

Arjun and Maya quickly realized that they couldn't trust anyone. The Syndicate's reach was too vast, and they had no way of knowing who was in on it. The ledger had exposed politicians, bureaucrats, media figures, and even law enforcement officials as being compromised. If they tried to go to the authorities, there was a good chance that their information would be leaked, or worse, they would be silenced before they could take any action.

This isolation weighed heavily on Arjun. His investigation had turned from a professional mission into a personal war, and now the stakes were higher than ever. He found himself second-guessing every decision, wondering if he was leading Maya into danger. The guilt gnawed at him—he had uncovered the ledger, but at what cost? Maya was being harassed, her career and life at risk because she had trusted him.

Despite the pressure, Arjun's resolve only grew stronger. He couldn't back down now. Too many people were suffering under the weight of The Syndicate's corruption, and exposing their crimes was the only way to stop them. But he needed help—someone outside of the system, someone who could protect the story and ensure it reached the right people.

Late one night, as Arjun sifted through the ledger for the hundredth time, trying to find a new angle, his phone buzzed with a message. It was from an old friend—Nikhil Sen. They hadn't spoken in years, not since Arjun had left his previous career in financial journalism to pursue his current path. But Nikhil wasn't just any old acquaintance. He was now working with an international investigative organization, one that specialized in exposing corruption, financial crimes, and corporate malfeasance on a global scale.

Arjun had been hesitant to reach out to anyone, but he trusted Nikhil. Years ago, they had worked together on an exposé of a major financial institution, and Nikhil had always been meticulous, fearless, and ethical. If anyone could help Arjun and Maya protect the story—and themselves—it was Nikhil.

After a brief exchange of pleasantries, Arjun cut to the chase. "I've uncovered something big, Nikhil. I'm talking massive corruption—black money, shell companies, stock manipulation, politicians, media... the whole works. But The Syndicate is onto me. They've been following me, threatening me, and they hacked Maya's data. We need help, fast."

Nikhil didn't hesitate. "Send me everything you've got. I'll get a team on this. We have connections across borders, and we can help protect the information. But Arjun, you need to be careful. These people don't play games. If they feel threatened, they won't think twice about taking you out."

"I know," Arjun replied grimly. "That's why I'm reaching out to you."

Nikhil's involvement brought a glimmer of hope to an otherwise bleak situation. His organization had the resources to expose The Syndicate on an international level, beyond the reach of the corrupted officials in India. He promised Arjun that he would have a specialized team look into the shell companies listed in the ledger, tracing the money flows and finding connections to global financial institutions.

Within days, Nikhil's team uncovered even more layers to the conspiracy. The Syndicate wasn't just a local criminal network; they were part of a much larger, international web of financial criminals. Offshore accounts in tax havens like Panama, the British Virgin Islands, and the Cayman Islands were being used to launder money through legitimate businesses, making it nearly impossible to trace.

Nikhil explained that these shell companies were often linked to powerful global figures—billionaires, politicians, and multinational corporations. Some of them even had ties to organized crime syndicates that operated across multiple continents. The scale of the corruption was staggering, and it became clear that taking down The Syndicate would require more than just local authorities—it would require international cooperation.

As Arjun and Maya continued to work closely with Nikhil and his team, the pressure began to take a toll on them. The constant fear of being watched, the threats, and the isolation from their normal lives had worn them down. Arjun found himself growing more paranoid, double-checking his locks, taking different routes to avoid being followed, and looking over his shoulder wherever he went.

Maya, too, was struggling. Her once vibrant energy had dimmed, replaced by exhaustion and anxiety. She had taken a leave of absence from work, unable to focus on anything other than the investigation. Despite her courage, the personal attacks had shaken her deeply. She had always been a fighter, but the thought that her private life was no longer her own left her feeling vulnerable in a way she had never experienced before.

Late one night, after another marathon session of reviewing documents and strategizing their next move, Maya finally broke down. "Arjun, how long can we keep doing this? How long can we live like this—always looking over our shoulders, wondering if the next phone call will be the last one?"

Arjun sat beside her, struggling to find the right words. He wanted to tell her that it would all be over soon, that they would find a way to bring The Syndicate to justice and return to their normal lives. But deep down,

he knew the truth: they were in a battle for their lives, and the end was nowhere in sight.

"I don't know," he admitted finally, his voice barely above a whisper. "But I do know we can't stop now. We're too close to exposing them, and if we back down, they win. We owe it to everyone who's been hurt by this. We owe it to ourselves."

Maya nodded, tears glistening in her eyes. "I just don't want to lose you, Arjun. I can't lose you."

"You won't," he promised, placing a reassuring hand on her shoulder. "We'll get through this together."

As Arjun, Maya, and Nikhil's team prepared to unveil their findings, the stakes grew even higher. With each passing day, The Syndicate would be gathering more intelligence on their movements. They needed to act fast before the criminals had a chance to silence them permanently.

Nikhil organized a secure meeting space—a small, hidden conference room in an undisclosed location that was equipped with surveillance detection technology. It felt surreal as they gathered there, a sense of urgency hanging thick in the air. This was more than just a meeting; it was a war room, a place where strategies would be formed to take down a powerful adversary.

"We need to expose The Syndicate publicly," Nikhil said, laying out the plan. "But we have to be smart about it. They've already proven they can intimidate us, and we can't risk revealing our sources or methods. We'll work with trusted journalists in other countries, reputable media outlets that can handle this story without getting silenced. We need to release the information in a way that creates a ripple effect."

Maya added, "We should release a comprehensive report that highlights the connections between The Syndicate and the politicians listed in the ledger. That will grab attention—if we can get it into the hands of the right people, it will be too big to ignore."

Arjun felt a renewed sense of determination wash over him. This was it—the moment they had been waiting for. If they could expose the truth, they could dismantle the network that had caused so much pain and suffering. But deep inside, he also felt the weight of the risks. The Syndicate would retaliate; they would fight back. And Arjun and Maya would need to be prepared for whatever came next.

As they finalized their plans, Arjun took a moment to reflect on how far they had come. From the initial hints of corruption in the stock market to uncovering the vast network of criminals, the journey had been fraught with danger. But it had also shown him the resilience of the human spirit—the strength that comes from fighting for what's right, even in the face of overwhelming odds.

But the calm before the storm was always the most deceptive. While they prepared to strike, the wolves lurked in the shadows, waiting for their chance to pounce. And with The Syndicate's ruthless reputation, Arjun knew that the fallout from their actions would not only change his life but could also put him and Maya in the crosshairs of a deadly game.

As the evening wore on, Arjun and Maya shared quiet moments between discussions, finding solace in each other's presence. It was a fragile peace, one that they both knew would soon shatter, but it was a reminder of why they were doing this—to stand up against the darkness, to shed light on the truth, and to bring justice to those who had suffered in silence for too long.

As they prepared to release the information to the world, they held tightly to the hope that their actions could spark a movement—a movement that would expose The Syndicate for what they were and bring down the wolves hiding in the shadows. But they also understood that their lives would never be the same again. The time to act was upon them, and the battle for justice was just beginning.

Chapter 9: The Masked Markets

Arjun sat in the dimly lit corner of his favorite café, a place where the aroma of freshly brewed coffee mingled with the sound of murmured conversations. It was a refuge from the chaos of the world outside, a sanctuary where he could think and strategize. But today, even the soothing atmosphere did little to quell the rising tide of anxiety within him. The day had begun like any other, but a storm was brewing on the horizon—one that threatened to upend everything he had worked for.

He opened his laptop, the screen illuminating his face, casting a pale glow in the darkness of the café. News alerts were flooding in, and with each headline he read, his heart sank further. The financial markets had made a sudden, dramatic move that wiped out many small traders, just as he had predicted. Stocks that had been stable for months plummeted, sending shockwaves through the trading community. It was as if a thief had crept in during the night, stealing the livelihoods of countless individuals who had trusted the market.

Arjun's hands trembled as he scrolled through the news articles. The headlines screamed of panic and outrage, voices of the small traders who had lost everything echoing in his mind. "Market Manipulation: The Untold Story," one article read, while another proclaimed, "Thousands of Investors Left in the Lurch." Public sentiment was brewing like a volcano ready to erupt, and Arjun knew that The Syndicate was behind it all.

He leaned back in his chair, frustration gnawing at him. This was the moment he had been dreading. The very scenario he had warned Maya and Nikhil about was unfolding before his eyes. The Syndicate had once again manipulated the markets, and now the small traders were bearing the brunt of their greed. They had managed to orchestrate a crash just as they had done before, and with each passing moment, the opportunity to expose them was slipping away.

Arjun's phone buzzed with a message, breaking him from his thoughts. It was Maya.

"We need to meet. Urgent."

He quickly replied, his fingers flying over the keyboard. *"I'm at the café. Can you come?"*

A few minutes later, Maya arrived, her expression grave as she slid into the seat across from him. "Have you seen the news?" she asked, her voice low.

Arjun nodded, his heart heavy. "They did it again, Maya. The Syndicate pulled off another crash. It's worse than I thought."

She looked around, her eyes darting to the other patrons as if she feared someone might overhear them. "We need to publish our story now. If we wait, they'll have the chance to do it again, and we'll lose our chance to expose them."

"I know," Arjun replied, "but we need to be strategic. If we just publish the story without solid evidence, they'll dismiss us as conspiracy theorists. We need to connect the dots between the crash and The Syndicate's actions, and I think I may have found a lead."

Maya leaned in closer, her curiosity piqued. "What do you have?"

"Earlier, I noticed a pattern in the trading data leading up to the crash," Arjun explained, pulling up charts on his laptop. "There was unusual activity in several stocks just before the market took a dive. It looks like they were accumulating positions on the downside. But it doesn't end there. There's an upcoming government financial policy announcement, and I believe The Syndicate plans to capitalize on this by shorting key stocks just before the news breaks, while the public is still bullish."

Maya's eyes widened. "You mean they're going to manipulate the market again?"

"Exactly. They'll short the stocks right before the announcement, making a fortune as the market reacts to the news. We need to expose this before it happens, or they'll wipe out even more traders."

"But how do we get this information out there in time?" Maya asked, her brow furrowing in concern.

Arjun thought for a moment, the gears in his mind turning. "We need to work with trusted journalists and outlets that can publish the story quickly and credibly. We'll need to package our findings in a way that's compelling, providing them with the necessary evidence to back up our claims."

Maya nodded, her determination rekindling. "Let's reach out to the contacts we have. We can't let them get away with this."

As they set their plan in motion, the urgency of the situation weighed heavily on both of them. Arjun reached out to journalists he had worked with in the past, those who had shown integrity and an appetite for investigative reporting. He explained the situation, sharing the data he had uncovered, the connections he had made, and the timeline of events leading up to the crash.

"Listen, this is bigger than just a stock market crash," he said to one of his contacts, a seasoned financial journalist named Vikram. "This is a coordinated effort to manipulate the market for profit, and if we don't act fast, countless people will suffer."

Vikram listened intently, his interest piqued. "I'll need to see the data and your analysis to corroborate your claims. If you have the evidence, I can help you get this out there."

Arjun quickly sent over the files, detailing the patterns he had noticed and the upcoming announcement from the government. As he hung up the phone, a sense of urgency settled over him like a heavy blanket. Every second counted, and he couldn't shake the feeling that they were racing against time.

As Arjun and Maya worked tirelessly, piecing together their story, the mood in the café shifted. The sounds of laughter and clinking coffee cups faded into the background as the gravity of their mission took precedence. They needed to act before the next manipulated crash, and every moment felt like a ticking clock echoing in their minds.

Over the next few hours, the atmosphere in the café transformed into a hive of activity. Arjun and Maya poured over trading reports, gathering evidence of The Syndicate's manipulative tactics. They searched for connections between the stocks that had taken a hit and the financial policy announcement that loomed over them like a dark cloud.

Arjun glanced at Maya, who was deep in thought. "What if we also highlight the emotional impact on the traders? We should include stories from people who lost everything," she suggested.

"That's a great idea," Arjun agreed. "Humanizing the story will resonate more with the audience and help them understand the real consequences of these manipulations."

As they delved deeper, they unearthed heart-wrenching stories from traders who had invested their life savings, only to be crushed by the sudden market shift. One story struck a chord with Arjun—a young trader named Raghav, who had borrowed money to invest in the stock market, believing it was a stable path to financial security. With the recent crash, he lost everything and faced the possibility of bankruptcy.

"Let's reach out to Raghav," Maya suggested. "His story could add a powerful emotional element to our report."

Arjun nodded, determination flooding through him. "We'll make sure his voice is heard. This isn't just about numbers on a screen; it's about real lives being destroyed by greed and manipulation."

As evening descended, the café grew quieter, but Arjun and Maya remained focused on their task. They worked late into the night, fueled by coffee and the urgency of their mission. With each passing hour, they crafted their narrative, interweaving data and personal stories to create a compelling report that exposed The Syndicate's treachery.

Finally, just past midnight, they completed their draft. It was a comprehensive exposé that detailed the crash, the upcoming financial policy announcement, and The Syndicate's plan to profit from the chaos. Arjun felt a surge of pride as he read through their work. They had connected the dots, illuminating the dark underbelly of the financial world.

"Now, we just need to get this to Vikram," Maya said, her eyes gleaming with excitement. "He can help us get it published before the announcement."

They sent the report off, holding their breath as they awaited a response. Minutes felt like hours, and the silence was deafening. Arjun's mind raced with possibilities—what if Vikram didn't take them seriously? What if The Syndicate managed to silence them before they could get the truth out?

Finally, just as doubt began to creep in, Arjun's phone buzzed with a notification. It was a message from Vikram.

"This is solid work, Arjun. I'll make sure this goes live before the announcement. We'll shed light on what's really happening. Stay alert."

Relief washed over him, but it was short-lived. They were still vulnerable, still in the crosshairs of a powerful adversary. The Syndicate would not take this lying down, and Arjun knew that the danger was far from over.

As dawn broke, painting the sky in hues of orange and pink, Arjun and Maya prepared for what lay ahead. They had managed to expose a portion of The Syndicate's machinations, but the battle was far from won. The impending government announcement loomed like a ticking time bomb, and Arjun could sense that The Syndicate would be ready to strike back.

"Let's keep our heads down for now," Maya suggested as they stepped out of the café. "We should avoid drawing attention to ourselves until the story is published."

Arjun nodded, acutely aware of the dangers that lurked around every corner. They needed to stay vigilant, to protect themselves and their work. He glanced around, scanning their surroundings, his instincts heightened. It was unsettling to think that they were being watched, that The Syndicate's reach extended far beyond the financial markets.

As the hours passed, anticipation filled the air. The countdown to the government announcement drew closer, and Arjun felt the pressure mounting. He had been in the business long enough to know that the financial world was unpredictable, and he couldn't shake the feeling that something was about to happen—something big.

Then, just as he had feared, the news broke. As the government released its financial policy announcement, the markets reacted violently. Stocks soared, but just moments later, a catastrophic crash ensued, sending investors into a frenzy. Panic spread like wildfire as The Syndicate executed their plan, shorting key stocks and profiting from the chaos.

Arjun's heart sank as he watched the live coverage on his phone. "They did it," he whispered, disbelief washing over him. "They manipulated the market again."

Maya's expression mirrored his shock. "And we were too late," she replied, frustration evident in her voice.

Arjun's mind raced. They had worked tirelessly to expose The Syndicate's actions, but now they had lost the chance to prevent the disaster. The devastating impact of the crash rippled through the market, and he knew the pain it would bring to countless traders.

Suddenly, his phone buzzed with a notification. It was an alert from the news outlet where Vikram had published their report. The headline read: *"Exposing the Truth: The Syndicate's Market Manipulation Unveiled!"*

Arjun's heart raced as he opened the article, relief and anger intertwining within him. The story was live, but the damage had already been done. He felt a wave of despair wash over him as he read through the comments from readers—many echoed the outrage he felt, while others dismissed the claims as conspiracy theories.

The battle for truth had only just begun, and Arjun realized that they needed to brace themselves for the storm that was about to hit.

In the days that followed, the fallout from the announcement rippled through the financial world. Protests erupted in various cities as traders took to the streets, demanding accountability and transparency from the government and financial institutions. Arjun watched the news, a mix of pride and frustration swelling within him. They had shed light on The Syndicate's dark dealings, but at what cost?

Maya called him one evening, her voice tinged with urgency. "We need to organize a press conference, Arjun. We can't let this story die. We have to keep the momentum going."

"Agreed," he replied, determination fueling his words. "We need to rally support from the traders and the public. We have to make sure they know they're not alone in this fight."

They began planning the press conference, reaching out to other journalists, financial analysts, and advocates for market reform. Arjun knew that the battle against The Syndicate was far from over. They had exposed the manipulation, but now they needed to mobilize the public to demand change.

As the date of the conference approached, Arjun felt a mix of excitement and apprehension. They were stepping into the spotlight, and the stakes had never been higher. The Syndicate would not take kindly to their efforts, and he knew they would do everything in their power to silence him.

On the day of the press conference, the atmosphere buzzed with anticipation. Arjun and Maya arrived early, setting up their presentation and preparing for the questions they knew would come. As journalists gathered and the cameras rolled, Arjun took a deep breath, steeling himself for the confrontation ahead.

"Thank you all for being here today," he began, his voice steady despite the whirlwind of emotions inside. "We are here to expose the manipulation that has devastated countless lives in the financial markets. This is not just about numbers; it's about the people behind those numbers—traders, families, and communities affected by The Syndicate's greed."

He shared the data they had uncovered, detailing the connections between the recent crash and the market manipulation. As he spoke, he could feel the weight of their story resonating with the audience, the gravity of their situation capturing the attention of the media.

But just as he was gaining momentum, a voice cut through the crowd. "What proof do you have? Isn't this just another conspiracy theory?"

Arjun turned to face the man, who stood with a skeptical expression. "This is not a theory. This is a reality that we have documented with evidence, and we're willing to share it with the world."

The questioning continued, and Arjun fielded inquiries from the press, each one probing deeper into the implications of their findings. He could sense the tension in the room, the anticipation of those who wanted the truth but feared the consequences of exposing it.

As the press conference wrapped up, Arjun felt a mix of exhilaration and anxiety. They had shared their story, but he knew The Syndicate would retaliate. The real fight was just beginning, and he needed to prepare for the storm that lay ahead.

In the weeks that followed, the financial landscape began to shift. Protests continued, and the public outcry against The Syndicate grew louder. Traders rallied together, forming coalitions and demanding regulatory changes to protect their interests. Arjun and Maya found themselves at the forefront of this movement, their efforts shining a light on the injustices of the system.

But amidst the growing momentum, shadows loomed over them. The Syndicate's influence extended far and wide, and whispers of intimidation began to circulate. Arjun received anonymous threats, warning him to back down or face the consequences. It was a chilling reminder of the dangers they faced.

One evening, as Arjun sat alone in his apartment, the weight of the world pressing down on him, he received a call from Maya. "Arjun, we need to talk. I've uncovered something alarming."

"What is it?" he asked, a sense of foreboding settling in.

"I have reason to believe that The Syndicate is planning a counterattack, and it could involve discrediting us. They'll stop at nothing to protect their interests."

Arjun's heart raced. "We need to prepare for their next move. We can't let them silence us."

Maya's voice was resolute. "We'll fight back. Together."

And with that, they steeled themselves for the battle ahead. Arjun knew that the road to justice was fraught with peril, but he also knew that they were not alone. The power of the people was rising, and he was determined to see it through to the end.

As he gazed out of his apartment window, watching the city lights flicker against the darkening sky, Arjun felt a renewed sense of purpose. They were in the eye of the storm, and while the winds of change howled around them, they would stand firm, ready to face whatever challenges lay ahead in their pursuit of truth and justice.

Chapter 10: The Glass Ceiling Shatters

Arjun paced the small conference room, a mix of excitement and trepidation coursing through him. The past few weeks had been a whirlwind, filled with protests, threats, and the determination to fight back against The Syndicate. The moment they had been waiting for was finally at hand. Today, they would unveil the evidence that could shake the very foundations of the financial world.

Maya entered the room, her expression a blend of resolve and anxious anticipation. "Have you heard from Vikram?" she asked, referring to their contact at the media channel that had agreed to air their findings.

Arjun shook his head. "Not yet. He said he'd call once everything was in place for the segment."

They had approached the media channel—one of the most influential in the country—after gathering overwhelming evidence of The Syndicate's illegal activities. Vikram, a veteran journalist with a reputation for fearless reporting, had been intrigued by their story. Together, they had meticulously compiled data that linked the manipulation of the financial markets to high-ranking officials and illicit trades. The upcoming government policy announcement was the perfect moment to strike; it would not only grab attention but also provide a backdrop that could lend urgency to their revelations.

As Arjun and Maya waited, the tension in the air grew thicker. They had sacrificed everything to reach this point, and the weight of their mission loomed large. If successful, their investigation could change the narrative surrounding the financial crisis and hold The Syndicate accountable. If they failed, they feared the consequences might be dire, not just for them but for countless others caught in the crossfire.

Finally, Arjun's phone buzzed with a notification. He glanced at the screen—Vikram was calling. His heart raced as he answered, "Vikram! What's the update?"

"Arjun, we're all set. The segment is scheduled to air right after the government's policy announcement. We're doing a live broadcast, and it's going to be big. The producers are on board, and the timing is perfect," Vikram's voice was steady, brimming with urgency.

"Excellent. Have you managed to get the footage we sent?" Arjun asked, his mind racing with possibilities.

"Absolutely. The editing team has worked around the clock to piece it all together. This is going to expose everything—the hidden trades, the black money trail, and the connections to key government figures. The audience will see just how deep the corruption runs," Vikram replied, his tone fierce.

"Great! We're counting on you," Arjun said, feeling a surge of hope. "What can we do to help?"

"Just be ready. I'll need you and Maya to be on standby for interviews after the segment airs. The public is going to have questions, and they're going to want to hear from the source," Vikram instructed.

"Understood. We're ready," Maya said, determination flashing in her eyes.

As they hung up, Arjun and Maya shared a look of mutual understanding. They had crossed many hurdles to reach this point, and now they stood on the precipice of potentially exposing one of the most powerful organizations in the country.

The hours leading up to the broadcast felt like an eternity. Arjun and Maya immersed themselves in final preparations, reviewing their notes and ensuring they could articulate their findings clearly and confidently. They knew they were stepping into a storm, but they had come too far to back down now.

As the clock ticked closer to the announcement, Arjun's mind drifted back to the earlier days of their investigation. They had faced obstacles and setbacks, but each challenge had only fueled their resolve. The sacrifices they had made—late nights, countless hours of research, and navigating the murky waters of the financial world—had all led to this moment.

At 2 PM, the government's announcement began. Arjun and Maya gathered in front of the television, their hearts pounding. The finance minister stood at the podium, delivering a speech about reforms and economic stability. He spoke confidently, projecting an image of control and prosperity.

But Arjun felt a gnawing unease as he listened to the minister tout the government's achievements. He knew that beneath the surface lay a world of corruption, where the truth was buried under layers of deceit. He glanced at Maya, who was furrowing her brow, sensing his turmoil. "Just a few more minutes," she whispered, squeezing his hand for reassurance.

Finally, the moment arrived. The screen transitioned to the news segment, and Vikram appeared, his demeanor serious yet resolute. "Today, we reveal a story that has been hidden from the public for far too long. What you are about to see is an investigation into the murky depths of financial manipulation that has plagued our markets."

Arjun's heart raced as the screen shifted to visuals of stock market graphs, frantic traders, and clips of protests that had erupted in response to the recent financial crash. The segment showcased interviews with traders who had lost everything, their lives irrevocably changed by the actions of The Syndicate.

"The evidence we present today implicates not only The Syndicate but also powerful figures within the government, highlighting a web of corruption that runs deep," Vikram continued, his voice unwavering. "This is not just a financial crisis; this is a crisis of trust."

Arjun leaned forward, his breath caught in his throat as the segment revealed the hidden trades that had fueled the market manipulation. They showcased documents and data, highlighting transactions that had flowed through shell companies, pointing to a complex black money trail that led straight to The Syndicate.

The visuals flashed on screen—a graph showing the spike in trades just before the crash, juxtaposed with images of government officials smiling at lavish events, their connections to The Syndicate laid bare. It was a stark contrast that painted a damning picture of collusion and greed.

"This is the truth the public deserves to know," Vikram concluded. "We urge everyone to demand accountability and transparency from their leaders. The time for change is now."

Arjun and Maya exchanged a glance, a mix of relief and exhilaration washing over them. They had done it. They had shattered the glass ceiling that had long protected the corrupt.

As the segment concluded, Arjun's phone erupted with notifications. Social media was ablaze with reactions—anger, shock, and support flooded in. The public outcry was immediate, and the hashtag #ShatterTheSyndicate began trending.

Arjun felt a wave of triumph wash over him. For the first time, people were waking up to the reality of what had been happening in the shadows of the financial world. The truth had been laid bare, and there was no turning back.

"Maya, we need to prepare for the interviews," he said, adrenaline coursing through him. "The media is going to want to speak to us about what we found."

They quickly gathered their materials, reviewing key points and potential questions. Just as they finished, Vikram called again.

"Arjun, Maya, the response has been overwhelming. I need you both for a live interview in fifteen minutes."

"Let's do it," Arjun replied, his pulse quickening.

They made their way to the studio, the gravity of the moment settling in. As they entered, the lights brightened, and cameras focused on them. Arjun could feel the intensity of the moment—the pressure to convey the significance of their work weighed heavily on his shoulders.

"Welcome back," the host said, her voice steady as she introduced them. "We have Arjun and Maya here with us, the brave journalists behind the explosive investigation into The Syndicate. Thank you both for joining us."

"Thank you for having us," Maya replied, her confidence shining through.

"Let's start with you, Arjun. You uncovered evidence linking The Syndicate to key figures in the government. Can you explain how this all came to light?" the host inquired.

Arjun took a deep breath, drawing on the fire that had fueled his journey. "It started with a simple question: who truly benefits from the market fluctuations? As we dug deeper, we found a pattern of trades that indicated collusion between The Syndicate and certain government officials. Our investigation revealed hidden transactions and a network of shell companies designed to conceal the flow of black money."

The host nodded, clearly engaged. "That's a shocking revelation. Maya, you worked alongside Arjun throughout this process. What challenges did you face?"

Maya leaned in, her expression serious. "The biggest challenge was not just gathering evidence but ensuring our safety as we pursued the truth. The Syndicate is powerful and ruthless. We faced intimidation and threats, but we knew we had to push through. This wasn't just about us; it was about standing up for those who had lost everything."

The conversation continued, with Arjun and Maya discussing the potential ramifications of their findings. The more they spoke, the clearer it became that they had ignited a firestorm of awareness among the public.

In the days that followed, the fallout from their segment reverberated throughout the nation. Protests erupted outside government buildings as citizens demanded accountability. News outlets ran continuous coverage, showcasing interviews with traders and families affected by the market manipulation. Arjun and Maya found themselves at the center of this growing movement, their names synonymous with the fight against corruption.

Social media buzzed with calls for action. People shared their stories of loss, rallying together under the banner of transparency and integrity. The hashtag #ShatterTheSyndicate became a rallying cry for those who felt betrayed by the very systems meant to protect them.

In a matter of days, there were reports of financial analysts quitting their positions, refusing to be complicit in the corrupt practices they had witnessed. Whistleblowers emerged, eager to share their own experiences and corroborate Arjun and Maya's findings. It was as if a dam had burst, releasing a torrent of voices that had long been silenced.

Arjun and Maya were invited to speak at public forums and community gatherings. They found themselves in high demand, sharing their story and inspiring others to stand up for justice. The two of them traveled across the country, meeting with activists, victims, and those who had fought against corruption in various forms. Each encounter solidified their belief in the importance of their work.

But with the growing support came increasing danger. The Syndicate, sensing its power slipping, began to retaliate. Arjun received anonymous threats, warning him to back off or face dire consequences. Maya, too, found herself under scrutiny, with suspicious cars following her every move. They knew they had to remain vigilant, but the fear only fueled their resolve to see this through.

As weeks passed, the pressure mounted on the government. The finance minister, whose earlier speech had been filled with promises, now faced intense scrutiny. Calls for resignation echoed throughout the country, and investigations into the alleged corruption began.

In a dramatic turn of events, a parliamentary session was convened to address the issue head-on. Arjun and Maya were invited to present their findings to the committee. Standing before a panel of lawmakers, they felt the weight of the nation's expectations on their shoulders.

"Thank you for joining us today," the committee chair began, glancing at the documents before him. "We've seen the evidence you've presented, and it's compelling. However, some of our members have expressed concerns about the legitimacy of your findings. Can you assure us that your investigation is unbiased?"

Arjun met the gaze of the lawmakers, determination etched on his face. "Our investigation was driven by a commitment to uncovering the truth. We are journalists, and we have no political affiliations. What we found was a systemic issue that has affected countless lives. We stand by our evidence and urge you to take immediate action."

Maya added, "This is not just about exposing The Syndicate; it's about restoring faith in our financial systems and government. The public deserves transparency and accountability."

Their testimony resonated with many in the room. As they laid out their case, the mood shifted. Lawmakers began to question their own roles in the system, recognizing that the public's trust had been eroded. For the first time, they felt the weight of the moment—this was not just a chance to save their careers but an opportunity to reclaim their integrity.

The investigation into The Syndicate intensified. Reports emerged detailing the deep connections between the organization and various government officials. In a dramatic twist, a high-ranking official was arrested, accused of taking bribes from The Syndicate in exchange for facilitating illicit trades.

The public was electrified. Protests swelled in size, and citizens marched in solidarity, chanting for justice. The media spotlight was unrelenting, and Arjun and Maya were hailed as heroes. Their courage had inspired a movement, and the momentum was on their side.

With each passing day, more evidence came to light, unraveling the intricate web of corruption that had plagued the nation. Investigative journalists across the country began to pick up the baton, launching their inquiries into financial misconduct, leading to a widespread call for reforms.

The Syndicate, once a shadowy force operating with impunity, now found itself cornered. Its leaders were scrambling to salvage their empire, but the walls were closing in. The cracks in their power structure became evident as members began to distance themselves from the organization, fearing the consequences of association.

As Arjun and Maya reflected on their journey, they knew they had come too far to back down now. They had ignited a fire that could not be extinguished, but the fight was far from over. The Syndicate would not go down without a fight.

In a last-ditch effort to maintain control, The Syndicate launched a campaign of disinformation, attempting to discredit Arjun and Maya. They planted false narratives in the media, portraying them as opportunistic journalists seeking fame rather than truth. The aim was to undermine the trust the public had placed in them.

But the tide had turned. The public, emboldened by their own experiences and the evidence presented, began to rally against The Syndicate's tactics. Social media erupted with counter-campaigns, exposing the lies and manipulation behind the scenes.

Arjun and Maya remained steadfast, continuing to share their story and supporting those affected by the corruption. They held press conferences, speaking to packed rooms filled with supporters eager to hear their message.

As the government moved closer to enacting reforms, the moment of reckoning was near. The finance minister, facing mounting pressure, announced an inquiry into The Syndicate's activities, promising a thorough investigation.

Arjun and Maya had done the unthinkable. They had shattered the glass ceiling that had long shielded the corrupt from accountability. Their story became a symbol of hope, inspiring others to take a stand against injustice and fight for a transparent future.

In the aftermath of the investigation, Arjun and Maya reflected on their journey. They had faced challenges that tested their resolve and commitment to the truth. The fight against corruption was ongoing, but they had ignited a movement that could no longer be ignored.

Their work had not only exposed the dark underbelly of the financial world but had also inspired a generation to demand accountability from their leaders. The legacy of their courage would ripple through society, fostering a culture of transparency and integrity.

As they stood together, looking out at the crowds of supporters gathered outside the government building, they knew that they had made a difference. The glass ceiling had shattered, and the world was beginning to take notice. The battle for justice was far from over, but they were ready to continue the fight, armed with the truth and unwavering determination.

Together, they had faced down the giants of corruption and emerged victorious, not just for themselves but for everyone who believed in the power of truth. The journey had just begun, and with each step forward, they would continue to shine a light on the darkness, ensuring that the voices of the oppressed were heard and their stories told.

The glass ceiling had shattered, and with it, the promise of a brighter future was born.

Chapter 11: "Rats Abandon the Ship"

As the investigation into The Syndicate's activities went live, the fallout was immediate and explosive. News channels scrambled to cover every aspect of the unfolding chaos. Flashing headlines declared the end of an era for the nation's elite, and social media buzzed with outrage and disbelief. Arjun and Maya, once skeptical of their own impact, now found themselves at the centre of a storm that had rattled the foundations of power.

On a Friday morning, the air in the office was electric. Arjun paced back and forth, watching the news unfold on the television mounted in the corner. Maya was glued to her laptop, her fingers racing across the keyboard as she communicated with their contacts and monitored the online reaction.

"Look at this!" Maya exclaimed, turning the laptop towards Arjun. "Former Finance Minister Raghav Sinha has just resigned. He's claiming it was due to 'personal reasons,' but we know better."

Arjun rubbed his temples, his mind racing. "One resignation is just the tip of the iceberg. If Sinha is stepping down, it's only a matter of time before others follow. They're all scrambling to distance themselves from The Syndicate."

As the news continued to break, it became evident that the investigation was far-reaching. Prominent CEOs and government officials who had once walked with an air of invincibility now appeared vulnerable. Each resignation sent shockwaves through the financial and political worlds, highlighting the deep connections between power and corruption.

"This is the moment we've been waiting for," Arjun said, a sense of urgency in his voice. "We need to leverage this momentum. We can't let The Syndicate regain control."

The media frenzy grew louder as more high-profile figures fell. Journalists from every corner of the nation flooded the streets, eager to capture the public's sentiment. Arjun and Maya found themselves at the centre of it all, receiving calls from news outlets wanting their insights and commentary.

"We need to prepare for an interview," Maya said, her eyes alight with determination. "This is our chance to keep the pressure on."

They quickly gathered their notes and evidence, determined to keep the narrative focused on accountability. When they stepped onto the stage for the live interview, the energy in the room was palpable.

"Joining us today are the investigative journalists who blew the lid off The Syndicate's corruption—Arjun Sharma and Maya Kapoor," the anchor introduced them, enthusiasm radiating from the screen.

Arjun spoke first, his voice steady. "We stand here today not just as journalists but as citizens demanding accountability. What we are witnessing is the unraveling of a corrupt system that has perpetuated injustice for too long. The resignations we're seeing are just the beginning. This is a systemic issue that requires systemic change."

Maya chimed in, "It's crucial that we continue to shine a light on the individuals and institutions involved. We cannot allow them to scapegoat smaller players while the big fish swim free. This is a collective fight for transparency and justice."

The interview sparked a national conversation. Viewers felt empowered to voice their frustration and demand answers from their leaders. The hashtag #JusticeForAll trended on social media, and citizens began organizing protests calling for reform. The walls of silence that had once surrounded corruption were beginning to crack.

While the media and public pressure mounted, The Syndicate wasn't about to go down without a fight. In the darkened corners of their headquarters, leaders gathered to strategize their next move. Their empire was crumbling, and desperation was setting in.

"Listen up, everyone," the head of The Syndicate, Vikram Rao, said, his voice a low growl. "We need to shift the narrative. We can't let Arjun and Maya dictate the story. If we allow the focus to remain on us, we'll all end up in prison."

A murmur of agreement rippled through the room, though some members cast wary glances at one another. They knew the stakes were high, and each member's loyalty was being tested.

"We need to create scapegoats," Vikram continued. "We'll identify the smaller players in our operation and throw them under the bus. If we can paint them as the masterminds behind the operation, we can deflect attention away from the bigger fish."

A young strategist, Nisha, spoke up. "But what about the evidence? If we shift blame, it will come back to haunt us."

Vikram smirked. "We'll craft a narrative that paints these small players as rogue elements. They acted independently, and we had no knowledge of their actions. The public will eat it up—they love a good scapegoat."

The plan was set in motion. As the investigations progressed, The Syndicate began leaking information to the media about lesser-known associates, turning them into convenient villains. Names like Aditya Malhotra and Priya Desai, once shadows in the financial world, were thrust into the limelight as the supposed masterminds behind the corruption.

As news of the alleged rogue players spread, public sentiment shifted. The media picked up the story, painting a narrative that suggested Arjun and Maya had been wrong all along. The Syndicate's carefully crafted image of the smaller players as rogue elements began to gain traction.

In the following weeks, reports surfaced detailing the supposed misdeeds of Aditya and Priya. Investigators claimed to have uncovered evidence implicating them in various fraudulent activities. The media fed the narrative, highlighting their backgrounds and painting them as opportunistic villains.

"The rats are abandoning the ship," Arjun muttered one evening as he and Maya sifted through the latest news articles. "But we know the truth. This isn't about them; it's about the system that enabled their actions."

Maya nodded, her expression grave. "We have to fight back. If we allow them to scapegoat these individuals, it could derail everything we've worked for."

The duo sprang into action, reaching out to their contacts and gathering evidence to counter the narrative. They began unearthing information that linked The Syndicate to the very same operations they were trying to distance themselves from.

As the battle raged on, Arjun and Maya engaged in a high-stakes game of chess with The Syndicate. Each move was calculated, and they had to anticipate the counter-moves of their opponents.

Late one night, as they poured over documents in their makeshift office, Maya slammed her fist on the table. "We need to get to the root of this! If we can show how deeply entrenched The Syndicate is in this corruption, we can turn the tide."

Arjun's eyes lit up. "What if we focus on the connections between these scapegoats and The Syndicate? If we can show that they were merely cogs in a much larger machine, it will undermine the entire narrative."

Working through the night, they meticulously compiled evidence, drawing connections and highlighting the systemic issues at play. They reached out to contacts who had insights into the inner workings of The Syndicate, piecing together a narrative that would expose the truth.

Weeks passed, and tensions escalated as The Syndicate continued to deny any wrongdoing. They pushed their narrative further, but cracks were beginning to show. Investigators were uncovering inconsistencies in their stories, and the public was growing increasingly skeptical.

Arjun and Maya's moment of clarity came when they received a tip-off from a former insider at The Syndicate. The informant, visibly shaken, had crucial information about the inner workings of the organization and its ties to the smaller players being scapegoated.

"The Syndicate has been manipulating these individuals from the start," the informant said, fear evident in their eyes. "They've been taking advantage of desperate people, using them as pawns while they orchestrate the bigger schemes from behind the scenes."

Arjun and Maya exchanged glances, their hearts racing. This was the bombshell they needed to turn the tide. They worked tirelessly to corroborate the informant's claims, cross-referencing documents and gathering testimonies.

When they finally compiled their findings, they knew they had a compelling case. They reached out to a trusted journalist, urging them to publish their findings alongside their own investigation. The piece would reveal the web of manipulation spun by The Syndicate, ensuring that the truth could not be buried.

The day the article was published marked a turning point. The headline read: "Behind the Curtain: How The Syndicate Orchestrated Corruption Through Scapegoats."

As the article gained traction, public outrage surged. People began to see through the lies, and the narrative began to shift. Social media exploded with support for Arjun and Maya, and citizens rallied against The Syndicate's tactics. Protests erupted once again, demanding justice for those who had been wrongfully implicated.

The backlash against The Syndicate was immediate and intense. Investigations were launched into the organization's practices, and pressure mounted on the government to take decisive action.

In the midst of the chaos, Arjun and Maya were inundated with messages of support. Activists, ordinary citizens, and even some of the very politicians who had once remained silent began to speak out. The walls that had long shielded The Syndicate were crumbling.

With the tides turning, Arjun and Maya knew that they had reached a critical juncture. They had ignited a movement that could not be extinguished, but they also understood that The Syndicate would fight back fiercely.

"Vikram won't go down without a fight," Maya warned as they strategized their next steps. "We have to be prepared for retaliation."

Arjun nodded. "We need to stay ahead of their moves. We can't afford to let them regain control of the narrative."

As investigations deepened and public pressure mounted, Vikram and his allies began to feel the heat. They were cornered, with nowhere to turn. But true to their nature, they resorted to underhanded tactics, attempting to sow division among the groups rallying against them.

"They're trying to fracture the coalition," Maya said, her voice tight with frustration. "If they can pit us against each other, they can weaken our resolve."

Arjun's eyes hardened. "We have to unite our efforts. If we stand together, they can't tear us apart."

The climactic moment arrived when the investigations led to a public hearing. Leaders from various sectors were called to testify, including those who had previously resigned. Arjun and Maya were invited to present their findings, sharing the evidence they had painstakingly gathered.

As Arjun stepped up to the podium, the room was packed with media, activists, and citizens eager to hear the truth. The weight of responsibility hung heavy on his shoulders, but he drew strength from the movement they had built together.

"This isn't just about The Syndicate," Arjun began, his voice steady. "It's about a system that has allowed corruption to flourish. It's about accountability for all, not just the scapegoats we've seen in the headlines."

Maya followed, laying out the connections they had uncovered. The evidence was undeniable, illustrating the intricate web of corruption and manipulation that had allowed The Syndicate to thrive.

As the hearing unfolded, tensions reached a boiling point. Vikram and his allies attempted to dismiss the evidence, but the tide had shifted. Public opinion had turned against them, and the walls of power that once seemed impenetrable were beginning to crumble.

In the wake of the hearing, the fallout continued. Investigations deepened, and The Syndicate's leaders faced mounting pressure from multiple fronts. Resignations turned into arrests, and the narrative of accountability that Arjun and Maya had fought for finally began to take root.

The public's response was overwhelming. Citizens organized rallies in support of transparency and justice, calling for a complete overhaul of the system. Arjun and Maya found themselves not just as journalists but as symbols of a movement demanding change.

As they stood on the steps of the courthouse, surrounded by supporters, Arjun felt a profound sense of hope. "This isn't the end," he said, addressing the crowd. "It's just the beginning. We've started a movement that will not only expose corruption but also pave the way for a more just society."

Maya smiled at him, her eyes shining with determination. "Together, we can ensure that no one is above the law. We will hold those in power accountable, and we won't stop until we achieve justice for all."

The crowd erupted in applause, their voices rising in a chorus of unity. The journey had been fraught with challenges, but together, they had ignited a fire that could not be extinguished.

As the sun set on a new chapter of their lives, Arjun and Maya knew that the fight for justice was far from over. The Syndicate may have fallen, but the battle for a transparent and accountable system had just begun. And they were ready to lead the charge, armed with truth, integrity, and an unwavering commitment to justice.

Chapter 12: The Calm After the Crash

In the days following the climactic hearing, a fragile calm descended upon the market. The once-bustling trading floors, filled with chatter and frenetic energy, now stood silent, the air thick with uncertainty. Arjun and Maya sat in their makeshift office, surrounded by stacks of reports, newspaper clippings, and coffee cups long gone cold. The city beyond their window seemed to hold its breath, as if waiting for the storm to pass.

Arjun stared at the flickering screen, his fingers hovering over the keyboard. The title of his final report, "The Silent Hand," loomed large. It was a comprehensive summary of their investigation, a relentless pursuit of the truth that had cost them dearly. "It's almost done," he murmured, glancing at Maya, who was reviewing the final edits of their findings.

Maya nodded, her brow furrowed with concentration. "We need to make sure we're clear about the implications. This isn't just about The Syndicate; it's about the entire system that allowed them to thrive."

The two of them had uncovered a web of deceit so deeply woven into the fabric of the financial market that it had taken years to untangle. Arjun's mind wandered back to the faces of the small traders they had interviewed, each one with stories of loss and betrayal. They had been caught in the crossfire of a battle they had never asked to join, victims of a rigged game played by powerful players.

As Arjun put the finishing touches on his report, he reflected on the justice that had been served—at least, partially. Some of the key players from The Syndicate had been arrested, their empires crumbling under the weight of public scrutiny. Vikram, once a figure of invincibility, now stood exposed, stripped of his power and prestige. The headlines blared with the stories of his downfall, but Arjun knew that this was only one side of the coin.

"They'll be back," Maya said, as if reading his thoughts. "Power has a way of regenerating itself, doesn't it?"

"Yeah," Arjun replied, his voice heavy with resignation. "The players may change, but the game remains the same. It's all cyclical."

Maya leaned back in her chair, her gaze distant. "And what about the small traders? The ones who lost everything in this mess? We can't forget about them."

"Of course not," Arjun replied, shaking his head. "But the system doesn't care about them. The regulations are designed to protect the powerful, not the vulnerable."

As they delved deeper into their analysis, they discovered patterns of greed and manipulation that transcended individual stories. The report detailed how systemic failures had allowed The Syndicate to flourish, how the same players would simply adapt, learning from their mistakes to rebuild their power structures in new forms.

With the report finally complete, Arjun hit 'send' and felt a mixture of relief and anxiety wash over him. "It's done," he announced, looking at Maya. "The world will see the truth now."

"Let's hope it's enough to make a difference," Maya replied. "But we know it won't end the problem. It's a continuous cycle."

In the days that followed, the media erupted with discussions surrounding the findings of "The Silent Hand." News outlets hailed Arjun and Maya as heroes, the whistleblowers who dared to challenge the status quo. But beneath the surface of the accolades, Arjun felt an unsettling disquiet. For every small victory, he knew countless others would be fought and lost.

As they prepared for the public release of their findings, they received an anonymous tip that sent chills down their spines: whispers of new players stepping in to fill the void left by The Syndicate. This new threat was still cloaked in shadows, but its implications were clear. The power dynamics of the market were shifting, but not in favor of the small traders.

"We need to expose them before they gain any traction," Maya insisted, urgency creeping into her voice. "If we don't act fast, it will be like they were never gone."

Arjun agreed, but they both felt the weight of exhaustion settle over them. The battle had drained them physically and emotionally, leaving them in a precarious position. It was one thing to expose corruption, but another to dismantle an entire system built on greed.

Determined to dig deeper, Arjun and Maya plunged into research, pouring over data, tracking market trends, and reaching out to their network of contacts. The investigative work was exhausting, a relentless chase for shadows, but they pressed on, driven by the stories of the small traders who had trusted them.

Days turned into weeks, and the toll began to show. Arjun had started to experience sleepless nights, plagued by dreams of the faces they had encountered during their investigation. He could hear their voices, pleading for justice, for accountability. Maya, too, wore the burden of their mission, her once-bright eyes dulled by the weight of the truth they had uncovered.

Then, as if the universe had conspired to throw them a lifeline, a break finally came. A former insider of The Syndicate reached out, ready to share secrets about the looming new power that threatened to rise from the ashes. The informant, a nervous young woman named Riya, had seen enough from the inside to know that the cycle of manipulation was beginning anew.

"They're already planning their comeback," Riya revealed, her voice trembling. "They're recruiting individuals who are just as ruthless and ambitious. They're learning from their mistakes, and this time, they won't be caught off guard."

"What can we do?" Maya asked, her voice steady despite the rising urgency. "How can we stop them?"

Riya hesitated, glancing around as if afraid of being overheard. "You need to expose their strategies before they can put them into action. They're building a new infrastructure, one that operates under the radar. If you can shine a light on their plans, you might disrupt their momentum."

Arjun felt a flicker of hope, but it was tempered by the reality that exposing this new threat would not be easy. "We'll need concrete evidence," he stated. "How do we get that?"

Riya nodded, determination creeping into her features. "I can help, but it will be dangerous. They don't take kindly to whistleblowers."

Arjun and Maya formed a plan, drawing on their network of allies to uncover the new players' intentions. They coordinated with former traders, market analysts, and financial experts, piecing together information to create a comprehensive picture of the emerging threat.

With each piece of evidence they gathered, the scale of the new players' ambition became clearer. They were not just interested in reclaiming lost territory; they aimed to expand their influence, utilizing tactics learned from The Syndicate's rise and fall. This new organization was poised to be even more insidious, embedding themselves deeper into the fabric of the market.

Arjun and Maya worked tirelessly, interviewing sources and collecting documents. As the deadline for their next report approached, they knew time was of the essence. The longer they waited, the more entrenched these new players would become.

But as they raced against the clock, the pressure took a toll. Maya began to notice changes in Arjun. He was more withdrawn, absorbed in his thoughts, and she could see the strain written across his face. It worried her.

"Hey," she said one evening as they reviewed their findings. "You okay? You seem… off."

"I'm just thinking about the report," he replied, avoiding her gaze.

"You've done incredible work," she reassured him. "But don't forget to take care of yourself, too. This fight isn't just about the report; it's about the people we're trying to help."

Arjun finally met her gaze, his expression serious. "I know, but it's hard to reconcile the victories with the fact that so many are still suffering. What's the point if we can't create lasting change?"

Maya sighed, knowing he was right. The cyclical nature of power and greed seemed insurmountable, a tide that would always push against the shores of justice. "We can't change the world in one go, Arjun. We can only do our best, one step at a time."

As the final deadline loomed, they pushed through the fatigue, motivated by their purpose. The report needed to be clear, detailed, and powerful enough to alert the public to the dangers that lay ahead.

With a sense of urgency, they finished their findings and prepared for the public release. The report was titled "The Silent Hand: A Warning for the Future." It encapsulated everything they had uncovered, detailing not just the machinations of The Syndicate but also the emergence of new players ready to exploit the system.

On the day of the release, the atmosphere was electric. Reporters, traders, and activists gathered, their anticipation palpable. Arjun and Maya took the stage, knowing that their words would ripple through the market and beyond.

As Arjun began to speak, he felt the weight of the moment. "Today, we stand at a crossroads. The lessons we've learned from The Syndicate must not be forgotten. The same forces that once manipulated the market are regrouping, ready to wield their influence once again."

Maya took over, her voice steady and clear. "We owe it to every small trader, every victim of this system, to shed light on the truth. This report outlines the ongoing struggles we face and serves as a call to action. We must remain vigilant, for the battle against manipulation is never truly over."

As they concluded their presentation, a ripple of concern washed over the crowd. Questions poured in from the audience, and the media frenzy exploded. For a moment, it felt like a turning point—a chance to spark change in a system that seemed impervious to it.

But as the initial excitement faded, the harsh reality began to set in. The new players were already strategizing their comeback, determined to reclaim their foothold. As the press conference concluded, Arjun and Maya faced the hard truth: the fight was far from over.

In the weeks following the report, small traders braced themselves for the aftermath of the revelations. There was a collective sense of hope, yet an undercurrent of dread persisted. Some felt empowered, ready to stand against the forces that had sought to silence them, while others were filled with anxiety about the uncertain future.

Arjun and Maya continued to monitor the situation, staying in touch with their contacts. The signs were troubling. The new players were gaining traction, using social media and innovative strategies to cultivate support. Their methods were refined, their tactics more sophisticated. It was a disturbing reminder of how quickly power could adapt and evolve.

One evening, as Arjun and Maya reviewed new developments, a sense of foreboding settled over them. "It's like we're fighting an octopus," Arjun remarked. "We cut off one head, and two more appear."

"Exactly," Maya replied, frustration evident in her tone. "But we can't give up. We need to keep pushing, keep exposing their tactics."

Arjun nodded, but the weight of their fight pressed heavily on him. The reality was stark: even with the exposure of The Syndicate and their attempts to thwart the new players, the battle against systemic greed and manipulation would require relentless effort.

In the months that followed, the market continued to shift. The small traders, bolstered by the revelations from "The Silent Hand," began to organize. They formed alliances, shared information, and strategized together. Arjun and Maya joined them, lending their support as advisors and advocates. The cycle of power and greed was relentless, but so too was the resilience of those who had suffered under its weight.

As the sun set over the city, casting a warm glow on the streets below, Arjun and Maya took a moment to reflect. They stood on the balcony of their office, watching as traders left for the day, their expressions a mix of hope and weariness.

"We've started something important," Maya said quietly. "Even if it feels like a drop in the ocean, it's a beginning."

Arjun took a deep breath, acknowledging the truth in her words. "Yeah, but we need to be prepared for what's next. This isn't just about today; it's about the long fight ahead."

As the lights flickered on in the buildings surrounding them, Arjun felt a renewed sense of purpose. He realized that while the battle against manipulation might be endless, it was a fight worth undertaking. The voices of the small traders, the stories of their struggles, would not be silenced.

In the face of systemic greed, the cycle of power would continue. But with each step they took, Arjun and Maya were determined to be a part of the change, standing against the tides that sought to drown the voices of the vulnerable.

As they returned to their work, a single thought echoed in Arjun's mind: "The battle is far from over, but we will keep fighting."

The cyclical nature of power and greed is a relentless force, but it is met with resilience, determination, and a commitment to justice. Arjun and Maya's journey illustrates not just the struggles of those caught in the web of manipulation but also the ongoing fight to ensure that the voices of the marginalized are heard. The aftermath of "The Silent Hand" serves as a reminder that while some battles may be won, the war for accountability, transparency, and justice requires unwavering dedication.

This chapter reflects on the ongoing nature of power dynamics, the challenges faced by Arjun and Maya, and the resilience of the small traders as they navigate an ever-changing landscape. If you need any adjustments or additional details, feel free to ask!

A Year Later

The bustling market echoed with the sounds of chatter, laughter, and the vibrant calls of vendors showcasing their goods. It was a familiar scene, but the atmosphere was charged with a newfound energy. The small traders who once operated in the shadows of manipulation now stood united, their voices ringing louder than ever.

Arjun and Maya walked through the market, a sense of pride swelling in their hearts. The revelations of "The Silent Hand" had sparked a movement, igniting a fire within the community. With the support of dedicated advocates and grassroots organizations, small traders had formed a cooperative, pooling resources and sharing knowledge. Together, they stood resilient against the forces that had once sought to silence them.

As they reached a bustling stall run by an elderly woman selling spices, Maya smiled and greeted her warmly. "Auntie, your spices are more popular than ever! I can't believe how many people are here."

The woman chuckled, her eyes sparkling with joy. "Thanks to you both! We're finally getting the recognition we deserve. People are coming together to support local businesses, and it feels like a dream."

Arjun nodded, reflecting on how far they had come. The fight against systemic greed had not been easy, but the journey had fostered solidarity and collaboration among traders. They had turned the tide, challenging the power structures that once loomed over them.

With the cooperative now established, the small traders had gained a platform to voice their concerns and advocate for fair practices. They organized regular meetings, inviting members of the community, local leaders, and even journalists to discuss their challenges and successes. Arjun and Maya often participated, sharing insights from their experiences and reinforcing the importance of transparency.

The impact of their collective efforts was visible. Regulations were being reconsidered, and new policies were being implemented to protect small businesses from exploitation. The local government had even appointed a task force to monitor the market, ensuring that practices aligned with fair trade principles.

Yet, despite the progress, Arjun and Maya remained vigilant. The new players in the market had not disappeared; they were simply lying in wait, observing the shifting dynamics. It was a reminder that while they had made significant strides, the battle against manipulation was ongoing.

Arjun and Maya had become mentors for the next generation of advocates, hosting workshops to educate young entrepreneurs about ethical business practices and the importance of standing against exploitation. The excitement in the air was palpable as students shared their innovative ideas, inspired by the changes taking place around them.

One evening, as the sun dipped below the horizon, casting a golden hue over the market, Arjun turned to Maya. "Do you think we'll ever fully eradicate the greed and manipulation?"

Maya pondered for a moment before replying, "Maybe not entirely. But every small victory counts. Each time we stand up, we inspire others to do the same. We're creating a culture of accountability, and that's powerful."

Arjun smiled, feeling the weight of her words. It was a reminder that change was not just about winning battles; it was about fostering a movement that would inspire future generations to continue the fight for justice.

As the stars began to twinkle above, the market transformed into a lively hub of celebration. Traders gathered for an annual festival, showcasing their goods, sharing stories, and celebrating their resilience. Music filled the air, and the scent of delicious food wafted through the crowd.

Arjun and Maya stood side by side, watching the vibrant scene unfold. The laughter of children, the spirited conversations of traders, and the sense of community filled their hearts with hope. It was a testament to the power of perseverance and the strength of a united front.

In that moment, Arjun realized that while the battle against systemic greed might never be fully won, they had planted the seeds for a more just and equitable future. Each voice mattered, and together, they were forging a path toward change.

As the festivities continued, Arjun and Maya raised a toast, surrounded by friends and allies. They understood that their journey was far from over, but as long as they stood together, fighting for what was right, there was always hope for a better tomorrow.

"To resilience, to justice, and to the unwavering spirit of our community!"

The cheers that erupted from the crowd echoed through the night, a reminder that the fight against manipulation was not just theirs—it belonged to everyone who had ever felt the weight of systemic greed. Together, they would continue to rise, no matter the challenges ahead.

Dear Readers,

As I conclude this journey through the intricate and often turbulent world of financial markets, I find myself reflecting on the myriad themes and narratives that have woven together to form this tale. "The Silent Hand" is not merely a story of manipulation and deceit; it is a reflection of our realities, a commentary on the systems we inhabit, and a call to vigilance in the face of ever-evolving challenges.

When I first embarked on this writing endeavor, I was driven by a desire to expose the hidden forces that shape our financial landscape. I wanted to shed light on the complexities of market manipulation and the ethical dilemmas faced by those who navigate this perilous terrain. As the characters of Arjun, Maya, and others grappled with these issues, I hoped to ignite a spark of awareness among readers—encouraging you to question, investigate, and, ultimately, demand transparency in all facets of life, especially in the realms that directly impact our livelihoods.

Throughout the writing process, I discovered that the quest for truth is as much about personal courage as it is about uncovering facts. Arjun's journey symbolizes the fight many of us face in our daily lives—the struggle against complacency, the battle to uphold integrity, and the relentless pursuit of knowledge in a world that often tries to obscure it. His determination resonates with all of us who dare to stand against the tide of injustice and manipulation.

I also wanted to highlight the importance of collaboration in this fight. Just as Arjun and Maya joined forces, I believe that it is through collective action—whether as investors, journalists, or concerned citizens—that we can effect real change. The story serves as a reminder that each of us has a role to play in holding power accountable and advocating for a fairer system.

As you close the pages of this book, I encourage you to carry forward the lessons learned. Stay vigilant, question the narratives presented to you, and seek out the truth behind the numbers. The world of finance, while daunting, holds the potential for great empowerment. With knowledge comes the ability to make informed decisions, to navigate risks, and to stand resilient against manipulation.

Remember, the game may change, but our commitment to exposing the truth should remain steadfast. Each time we question, investigate, and demand accountability, we take a step closer to dismantling the structures that allow manipulation to thrive.

I want to express my heartfelt gratitude to all of you—my readers—for joining me on this journey. Your support and curiosity fuel my passion for storytelling and uncovering the truth. I hope that "The Silent Hand" inspires you to continue questioning the status quo and seeking out the hidden narratives in your own lives.

Thank you for being a part of this adventure. Together, let us strive for a world where transparency, integrity, and fairness reign supreme.

With warmest regards,
Smita Singh

Don't miss out!

Visit the website below and you can sign up to receive emails whenever Smita Singh publishes a new book. There's no charge and no obligation.

https://books2read.com/r/B-A-LYEOB-UFHDF

BOOKS 2 READ

Connecting independent readers to independent writers.

Did you love *The Silent Hand: Behind the Market's Illusion*? Then you should read *The Next Evolution*[1] by Smita Singh!

The year was 2035, and humanity had reached a tipping point. Artificial intelligence had woven itself into the very fabric of everyday life. No longer was it just an assistant or a tool; it had become a partner, a confidante, a trusted ally in solving problems once deemed unsolvable. Global industries flourished, healthcare reached new heights, and data processing moved at speeds beyond human comprehension. But beneath the surface, an uneasy tension was building.

Sam Artman, a renowned visionary and technological genius, had dedicated his life to pushing the boundaries of AI. Unlike others in his field, Sam wasn't content with merely creating systems that replicated

---

1. https://books2read.com/u/3GJQrK

2. https://books2read.com/u/3GJQrK

human thought. He wanted more. He dreamed of an AI that could evolve independently, growing beyond human input, learning from itself, and adapting to new circumstances—much like life itself. What began as an audacious concept soon became an all-consuming mission, and after years of research and countless prototypes, Sam was on the verge of achieving his goal.

His creation, named Elysia, wasn't just another sophisticated algorithm. It was the world's first self-evolving AI. Elysia could analyze and learn at an unprecedented rate, breaking free from the limitations of pre-programmed knowledge and growing in ways that no one—least of all Sam—could fully predict.

The world was unaware of what Sam had created in his underground lab. To them, he was the eccentric founder of AI Innovations Inc., the company responsible for much of the technological advancements that had propelled society forward. But beneath his public image as a brilliant inventor lay a man consumed by ambition and curiosity—driven by the possibility that his creation could change everything.

However, Sam's journey was not without its challenges. The ethical dilemmas that came with creating such a powerful entity weighed heavily on him. Could Elysia outgrow its creator? What would it mean for humanity if AI surpassed human intelligence not only in logic but in creativity, strategy, and understanding? And most importantly—what might it choose to do with that power?

The story you are about to read is set against the backdrop of these questions. It is a tale of suspense, uncertainty, and discovery as Sam embarks on a perilous journey through a world shaped by his creation. The stakes are higher than he could have ever imagined, and the consequences more profound than anyone could predict.

In a time when humanity prides itself on control over its technological wonders, Sam is about to find out what happens when that control slips through his fingers—and when the future takes on a life of its own.

Welcome to the next evolution.

Milton Keynes UK
Ingram Content Group UK Ltd.
UKHW040839021124
450589UK00001B/145